473

MAGIC BY THE BOOK

NINA BERNSTEIN

MAGIC
BY THE
BOOK

PICTURES BY **BORIS KULIKOV**

FRANCES FOSTER BOOKS
FARRAR STRAUS GIROUX · NEW YORK

www.fsgkidsbooks.com

Library of Congress Cataloging-in-Publication Data
Bernstein, Nina, date.
    Magic by the book / Nina Bernstein ; pictures by Boris Kulikov.— 1st ed.
        p. cm.
    Summary: After returning from a trip to the library, eleven-year-old
Anne and her younger brother and sister discover a magic book which
sends them on amazing adventures where they meet Robin Hood, giant
bugs, and a dark, sinister man with a wolfish face.
    ISBN-13: 978-0-374-34718-5
    ISBN-10: 0-374-34718-2
    [1. Magic—Fiction.   2. Space and time—Fiction.   3. Characters in
literature—Fiction.   4. Books and reading—Fiction.   5. Brothers and
sisters—Fiction.   6. Robin Hood (Legendary character)—Fiction.
7. Insects—Fiction.   8. Werewolves—Fiction.]   I. Kulikov, Boris,
date, ill.   II. Title.

PZ7.B4568Mag 2005
[Fic]—dc22
                                                                2004043329

To David and Daniel, to Lynn and Paul,
and in memory of Danny, who was in the garden, too

CONTENTS

MAGIC BY THE BOOK

THE BEGINNING

Dusk, the long blue dusk of summer, was already falling on the garden by the time they discovered the book. It was a small, shabby volume lying at the bottom of the wicker basket. Its color was indistinguishable in the deepening twilight, and the faded gilt lettering on its spine was illegible.

Neither Anne nor Emily remembered choosing it at
the library that afternoon. Perhaps their younger brother,
Will, had scooped it up by mistake before running off to
join the ball game in their neighborhood's last vacant lot.
The three children had filled the basket to the brim with
books, greedy for the long, lazy days of reading ahead. The
basket had bumped against the girls' bare legs as they carried it home between them. They had stopped to rest and
rummage and compare finds every block or so. But this
book must have stayed wedged at the bottom, unnoticed.

Settled in the cool shade of the green hammock on
their return, Anne and Emily had read all afternoon, with
no more than the rustling leaves of the copper beech tree
to disturb them, and sometimes, in the distance, the cry of
boys playing ball. Even Will, who was six and three-
quarters, had not come back begging them to read him a
story. Gradually the basket had emptied and the hammock had filled, until it cradled a score of books besides
the two girls.

Anne, tall for eleven, was at one end, scrunching up
her skinny shins to make room. Nine-year-old Emily
curled at the other end, wiggling her toes from time to
time in the exquisite knowledge that the summer had
only just begun, even if the day was drawing to a close.

By the time they caught sight of the book, both glancing down to the basket in the grass at the same moment, they knew their mother's voice would soon be echoing out over the hollyhocks from the first lighted window, calling them in to set the table for supper. Strangely excited, they plucked the book from the basket. Sitting side by side now at the edge of the canvas hammock, they opened it to the first page and began to read.

"Dusk, the long blue dusk of summer, was already falling on the garden by the time they discovered the book," they read. "It was a small, shabby volume lying at the bottom of the wicker basket . . ."

There on the yellowed page were their names, their ages, their hammock, and their copper beech tree.

"Anne, it's magic, it just has to be magic," Emily whispered, looking into her sister's face. Pale under her freckles in the fading light, Anne hushed her and turned the page.

"As they sat reading, the tall pines at the bottom of the garden filled with mist. White and thick, it swirled up the slope to meet them, obscuring arbor, apple tree, azaleas, until only the tops of the trees were visible, knit by the fog into a forest. And from this forest suddenly there came the sound of approaching hoofbeats."

Even as they read the words, Anne and Emily heard the sound, muffled at first, but unmistakable and coming closer: a horse's hooves on the forest floor. Starting up with a cry, Emily was enveloped in the mist she had just read about, and clutched for her older sister's hand. The book tumbled to the ground, and the two girls found themselves alone in a fog-shrouded forest clearing, braced for the galloping horse and rider to burst upon them.

SHERWOOD IN THE TWILIGHT

$\mathcal{B}$ig and black, the horse hurtled through the trees, so close to them that they screamed. It shied away and reared, and the rider swore, his voice harsh, his black-gloved hands straining at the reins. Looming high above Anne and Emily in his dark, hooded cloak, he looked down at them and swore again.

"Struth, all Saxon brats should be drowned like kittens at their birth," he spat out. "Always in the way. And yet, perhaps you two can be of some use. Answer me quick, the shortcut to Nottingham, is it not this way?"

The girls just gaped at him, eyeing the sword hilt that gleamed at his side where the cloak fell back.

"Come, come!" he shouted. "I have no time to waste. Is there not an inn nearby, called the Sherwood Arms or Battling Boar? Surely I am not far from the high road here."

Instinctively, the girls looked over their shoulders, to where their big brown-shingled house should have stood, solid and comforting, at the top of the garden hill. There was nothing there but trees, mist, and deepening shadows.

Suddenly, Anne knew where they were. The words of a poem she had read and reread came back to her, so vividly that she could almost hear them whispered through the little glen.

> Sherwood in the twilight, is Robin Hood awake?
> Grey and ghostly shadows are gliding through the brake,
> Shadows of the dappled deer, dreaming of the morn,
> Dreaming of a shadowy man that winds a shadowy
>   horn.

"Em, we're in Sherwood Forest." Anne breathed the words out slowly. Her dark eyes glowed; her hand squeezed her sister's so hard it hurt.

A small part of Emily wanted to pull away her hand and run. For an instant she wondered if she could break through the mist to the empty lot around the corner. Surely Will must be there with his buddies, chasing pop flies through the weeds.

Even when Sherwood Forest was just make-believe, even when their magic adventures were yearnings and playacting, Anne was sometimes too intense for Emily. Every so often Emily would have preferred to run off by herself to climb a tree or play an uncomplicated game of tag with children her own age. But that year the boys in her class had decided that all girls were aliens, even a tomboy like Emily. By spring the other girls seemed to have abandoned running games at recess for whispering in impenetrable circles. And Anne needed her more than ever—as audience, collaborator, and supporting cast rolled into one.

A year and a half had passed since the family's return to America from England, where they had lived in London for three years. But Anne still felt like a stranger among her classmates. It didn't help that her homeroom teacher, Mrs. Feathersnee, never stopped saying things like, "Class, let's hear Anne Thornton pronounce that word the *British* way," or, "I'm sure *Anne* knows the answer," or even, once, remarking on Anne's braids and blue jumper, "Ooooh, how *European!*"

It didn't help that the children's father, who worked for a newspaper, had been seen picking them up in a dusty, dented car with the steering wheel on the wrong side. Or that when the PTA ladies came to call, the children's mother was planting bulbs in the rain, still in pajamas under a muddy slicker, her mind on the gardening column she had to write that afternoon. Moreover, since the PTA had been expecting cupcakes for the bake sale, it was most unfortunate that Will happened to wander by holding the rusty muffin tin that housed his worm and dirt collection.

Even in those days (more than forty-five years ago, now—perhaps before your own parents were born), not many rambling old properties like the Thorntons' remained in Whitestone, Queens, which is part of New York City. Such places were oddities amid the new developments of identical side-by-side houses and tidy lawns. And the children quickly realized that their family was something of an oddity, too. As a rule, boys didn't seem to care; certainly Will never lacked for playmates. But in Anne's grade, many girls were ready to giggle behind their hands at anyone who didn't fit in.

The snickers in class soon turned to cold shoulders in the schoolyard. Anne, who had been "that *American* girl" at her London school, didn't mind much. Standing alone at the chain-link fence during recess, she would lose herself in a book, looking up only to catch Emily's eye across the asphalt. Later, the house and garden would be waiting like a stage set for their own version of the plot. They might ransack the attic for bits of costume and draft Will to play, too; or they might just wrap themselves grandly in imaginary cloaks.

But now, glancing at each other, they saw that hooded brown cloaks really covered their hair and fell away from green jerkins. Their feet and legs were no longer bare, but shod in leather and brown hose. Like Anne's, Emily's heart leaped at the possibilities.

Then the crack of the man's riding whip made both girls cry out and cringe.

"Half-wits!" he screamed, flailing at them. His own rising fear of having gone astray in the forest, and so near to nightfall, spurred his fury. His hood fell back, and they saw his face: the eyes deep set, and a cruel, twisted scar above the mouth, not quite hidden by a dark mustache. "Saxon dogs!" he shouted.

"Dog yourself," retorted Emily, stung out of the daze that had possessed both sisters. She reached for the riding crop as he brought it down, and wrenched it from his grasp.

"I'll teach you to go around trying to hit people and run them over with your horse, you big brute," she said.

"I'll bet you're one of those evil Normans, always stomping on peasants and lording it over the Saxons. Just wait. Robin Hood'll show you!"

At the sound of the name, the man's face changed. "Outlaw whelps, are you?" he said. "I'll not waste whipping on the likes of *you*."

He reached for his sword. The metal gleamed cold and hard in the last light of day as he pulled it from the scabbard.

Anne grabbed Emily's arm and tried to pull her out of his reach. Why, she wondered, did her little sister always have to be so rash? She was going to get them killed before they even got their bearings.

But the dark knight's blade was not halfway unsheathed when an arrow sang through the trees and transfixed his hand. He cried out, then, with a quick glance in the direction from which the arrow had come, wheeled his horse around and spurred it the other way.

He had barely gone two strides when three figures in Lincoln green dropped from the trees and blocked his path.

"Not so fast, sirrah," said the tallest, taking firm hold of the horse's bridle. "After that bold attack on children, a man such as yourself surely grows faint and needs rest and refreshment."

"And has the means to pay for it," added the second, a short, stocky man with a gray beard. He hefted the stranger's saddlebag and smiled broadly at the jingling sound it made.

The rider grabbed back the reins. Kicking the horse, he threw his weight to the right, and tried to force the animal past the third member of the green-clad band, a slender, beardless youth.

"Nay, sir knight," said the youth, laughing as he dodged the horse's flank, and with a quick tug and a twist of the rider's cloak, he brought him somersaulting out of the saddle. "No need to dismount with such haste. You might hurt yourself.

"Why, Scarlet," the youth continued, turning to the tall man, at whose feet the rider had fallen in a groaning heap, "I do believe the gentleman wished to offer his mount to his young foes here."

Scarlet soothed the horse, and led it back to where the girls still stood, Emily grinning from ear to ear, Anne with a shiny-eyed, almost worshipful look on her face.

"My master will want to meet such stalwart lasses," Scarlet said. "Will you not come dine with Robin Hood in the greenwood tonight?"

They looked quickly at each other. This was no time to turn back. "Yes," they breathed together. "Yes, please."

"Good, that's settled," he said. He turned his attention to the knight, now struggling to his feet. "Come, sir knight, since we are to be traveling companions, let us be better acquainted. Will Scarlet's my name, and this stout-hearted fellow is Arthur-the-Bland—tut, tut, don't let his gray beard misguide you," he went on, as the angry knight tried and failed to break the older man's grip on his arm. "Nor should you misjudge Alan-a-Dale by his beardless cheek," he added as the youth neatly relieved the knight of his sword and dagger. "And who would you be, traveling with such haste through our forest this evening?"

" 'Tis no forest of yours, but Prince John's," retorted the glowering knight. "He is my liege lord, and I, Sir Reynold Pomfret, ride on his business. Let me go, or 'twill go badly for you all, and worst for your master, the traitor Robin Hood."

"No traitor," Alan-a-Dale said coolly, "but rather a loyal subject to our King, Richard the Lion-Hearted, who even now is traveling back to us from the Holy Land, men say."

"Hah, say what they will, he'll not be back," Sir Reynold Pomfret sneered, and a strange smile twisted the scar under his mustache.

"Enough," roared Scarlet. "Bind his hands and tether him to his horse. Let him walk behind while these fine lasses ride before him."

Scarlet's strong hands lifted Emily and then Anne to the wide saddle, while Alan-a-Dale tied and leashed the angry knight, who was soon breathing too hard to curse.

Deeper into the forest they turned, Scarlet leading the horse with a firm hand and a quick stride, and the other men walking on either side of their prisoner to keep him in check.

"Anne, it's really happened, hasn't it," Emily whispered, half turning in the saddle to seek her sister's familiar face, snub-nosed and freckled under her hood. "But how?"

Even in the near darkness, Emily could see Anne frown.

"Don't even ask," she hissed back. "It might stop!"

By now the night had truly fallen, and the path was hard to follow. The tangle of roots underfoot and the overhanging branches sometimes seemed to bar the way completely. But Will Scarlet always managed to bring the stallion around the obstacles, with gentling noises that Anne and Emily found a comforting counterpoint to the strange sounds of the forest.

How could he possibly find his way? Emily wondered. Three times he stopped and felt a tree trunk before turning right or left, but to the girls' eyes, straining through the dark, one tree was exactly like another. Once, the glitter of a brook broke the darkness, and they realized the bits of sky showing through the trees were pierced with stars. The fog had rolled away, and from time to time amid the branches they glimpsed a crescent moon. Finally they came to a halt in a small clearing, and Alan-a-Dale gently blindfolded Anne and Emily, while Arthur-the-Bland tended to Pomfret—for the approach to the outlaws' camp had to stay secret.

For a moment, Anne thought she smelled earth and dampness, as though they were passing through a cave. Emily was aware of nothing more than the linen blind-fold's scent of pine. The horse's hooves seemed to strike rock for a stretch, and then were again muffled in the grass.

Alan-a-Dale began to sing a sweet, thin tune that echoed in the night. *"It was na in the hall, the hall, / Nor in my lady's bower, / But it was in the good green wood . . ."*

Suddenly the tune came back, rich with many voices and the sound of laughter. *"There's many that speaks o' Robin Hood, / Kens little where he was born."*

There were cries of greeting, a flash of torches, a clat-ter of arms. Many hands reached to help Anne and Emily dismount. Squinting in the bright firelight when their blindfolds were lifted, the girls found themselves in the midst of a merrymaking crowd. One big fellow in a leather jerkin had what looked like a roasted chicken leg in one hand, one strummed a lute, and several lifted tankards to their lips. Behind them lay a long trencher table laden with food and drink, and beyond that, a haunch of venison sizzled on a spit over an open fire.

Then the crowd parted, and a tall, handsome man walked toward them. Eyes twinkling, he swept his cap from his head and bowed.

"Welcome to Sherwood," he said. And cocking an eyebrow at Scarlet, he added, "What company is this you bring to share our feast, Will? Two lasses of tender years and one scowling knight?"

"Yes, master," said Scarlet. "But the knight comes with heavy saddlebags, and travels on mysterious business, and the lasses are brave beyond their years."

Scarlet added a few more words in a whisper, and Anne and Emily, trying to look modest, saw the outlaw chief's handsome face darken. Then he smiled again, and, taking Anne's hand, lightly kissed it.

"Robin of Locksley, at your service," he said.

It was a moment Anne would never forget. But it was rudely cut short by a snort from Pomfret.

"Locksley Hall is but a ruin," he jeered, "and Locksley lands are fallen to Guy of Guisborne. As much say Robin of Locksley as Robin of Naught."

The contempt on his face showed plainly in the

torchlight, and there was a sharp intake of breath, like a low whistle, from the men. One bent and grizzled fellow made as if to throttle Pomfret.

"A pox on thee for a foul thief," he growled. "I'll make thee bow to thy better! Call him Robin o' Locksley or Robin Hood, he's worth ten score of Guisbornes!"

Robin shot out an arm and held the old man back.

"Nay, Thomas, only five score Guisbornes, surely," he said lightly. "Come, let's to dinner. Perhaps some food and drink will put our guest in better spirits."

Taking Emily on one arm and Anne on the other, he led them toward the long oak table where the others were gathered.

Just then a slender figure in green rode out of the woods, with a fat kirtled abbot slung across the horse like a sack of flour.

"Set another place, Robin," sang out the rider. "I have here a guest who can pay dearly for his supper—aye, and unburden his guilty conscience by making large gifts to the poor, too."

"Well met, Marian," cried Robin, catching her in his arms as she dismounted, and slipping off her green hood so a wave of dark hair fell upon her shoulders. "Presently you shall tell us how you came upon this fine, round spec-imen of an abbot, as fat from the eating of his peasants' grain as they are thin for want of it, I'll wager."

Anne barely had time to hope that she wasn't gawking at the pair as much as Emily, when the crowd closed around them and the feast began in earnest: roasted meats, potatoes cooked in embers, wild berries, great wheels of yellow cheese, hunks of bread, and cool drafts of a honey drink called mead that made one's head spin most pleasantly.

Pomfret and the abbot ate, too, but with sour faces. Flanked by Arthur-the-Bland and Will Scarlet near the end of the long table, they seemed to be serving as the butt of many uproarious jests. But after the ballad singing began, they were forgotten.

Once, under cover of the laughter that Alan-a-Dale won with his rendition of "The Ballad of Robin Hood and the Monk," Pomfret began whispering in the abbot's ear, urgent and intense. Anne watched the abbot's face become an open-mouthed caricature of surprise. He gave a quick glance around the table, and when his eye met hers, he bleated a nervous laugh and said something to Pomfret out of the corner of his mouth.

Anne kicked Emily under the table. "Em, look, they're plotting something. I'm sure of it. You keep watch. I'm going to eavesdrop if I can."

"No fair," said Emily, nursing her ankle. "Let me go. I'm a better size for it." And before Anne could dispute the point, Emily had ducked under the table.

*

For a moment Emily crouched there, disoriented by so many legs and leather-shod feet in the flickering firelight. The raucous chorus of voices echoed in her ears. Then she spotted the abbot's gown and surplice, and recognized Pomfret's black boots. Crawling under the center of the table, and dodging a few inadvertent kicks, she drew near enough to hear the abbot belch and Pomfret swear.

"Struth, man, can't you understand why Prince John must hear the news first, and the quicker the better? This is the chance he's been hoping for. Deal with the matter forcefully, and the Lion-Heart need trouble him no more than a kitten in an unwanted litter. Wait, and word of Richard's capture will spread to men like these. Then we'll see no end to collecting ransom and fomenting resistance."

The abbot's white hands fluttered in his lap, and he pressed them together.

"But surely it would be unwise to attempt an escape tonight, Sir Reynold. In the dark? Through unknown woods where yet more brigands may lurk? I'm not a well man, you know. Subject to palpitations."

"That might be the very thing for a diversion," Pomfret shot back. "Extra fancy palpitations, perhaps a few convulsions. You can drool, can't you? Leave the rest to me."

Before the abbot could protest, Emily saw Pomfret reach under the table and punch him hard in the solar plexus, knocking the wind out of him. The abbot gasped like a beached whale. The knight's timing had been perfect—the song was over, the applause dying down in anticipation of the next ballad.

"Convulsions!" he called out loudly. Emily saw him thrust a leg behind the fat man's feet and tip him up, so that, still struggling for breath, the abbot lost his balance on the bench and fell backwards.

"Watch out, he's trying to escape," Emily cried. "It's just a trick!" But muffled by the heavy table, her voice was lost in the commotion that followed. By the time she emerged from the thicket of legs, Pomfret had disappeared.

And so had Anne.

CAPTURED

$\mathscr{A}$ few paces from the fire-lit circle of Robin's band, the forest seemed very dark indeed. But Anne ran on, determined not to let Pomfret escape. She felt the importance of stopping him like a terrible weight in her chest, though she could not have explained why.

She searched her memory in vain for a Reynold Pomfret in all the Robin Hood stories she knew. If she and

Emily had stepped into one of the old tales, surely she should recognize him and know the role he was supposed to play. Perhaps this was one of the lost ballads, uncollected and unknown. Perhaps it was a brand-new plot, unfolding without any certainty of a happy ending. Either way, she felt, her actions would count—and her inaction, too.

Calling out to the others when she first saw Pomfret slip away, she had not waited to see if they heard her or were following. Now the voices had faded, and the sound of Pomfret's boots no longer echoed ahead. In the pale light of the crescent moon, she saw nothing but black branches and thick underbrush on all sides. She paused to listen, and the sound of her own breathing suddenly seemed very loud.

Then from behind her came the crack of a dead branch underfoot, and before she could whirl around, she found herself pinioned, a black-gloved hand stifling her cry.

"The meddling maiden," Pomfret growled in her ear. "Well, well. You shall serve my purpose yet."

✳

Back in the glen, the tumult was broken by a sharp whistle, as Robin Hood called his followers to order.

"Ho, Scarlet, Roger, Much, and you, Isaac, give chase

to the dark knight—he cannot have gone far. You others there, stand watch at Owl Hill. In case he proves too fleet for Scarlet's band, you can catch him in the gully. He'll find it no easy matter to give us the slip in our own Sherwood, and on a moonlit night at that."

Then he turned to Emily and gently put a hand on her shoulder. "Now, my young friend. What's this about a plot?"

It was the kindness in his voice that did it. Suddenly Emily felt tears fill her eyes, and she couldn't trust herself to speak. With Anne there, it was easy to be the rash, outspoken one, Miss Reckless and Feckless, as her father teasingly called her. Now Anne had vanished, leaving Emily adrift in the adventure alone.

For the first time since she had looked back to find the house and garden gone in a swirl of mist, Emily was gripped by panic. *This isn't real*, she told herself, trying to still the fear that threatened to engulf her. But what was real?

She cast back for the images of everyday life.

Her mother, dark curly hair still uncombed, cutting rain-rumpled peonies before breakfast. Her father, feet up on the porch rail, glasses slipping down his nose, declaiming from the Sunday paper. Her brother, Will, small for six, crawling triumphantly out from behind the compost heap with a lost baseball in hand and his fair, straight hair layered with earthworms and ancient grass clippings.

But they seemed almost like images from a favorite book, no more real than the torch-lit band encircling her now, or the vast darkness of Sherwood Forest into which Anne had vanished.

For this was the kind of enchanted adventure they had always dreamed about when they searched the attic for a secret door into the past, or unearthed old coins and marbles from the flower beds, trying to believe they were magic talismans. They had yearned for magic as strong as the spell cast by the books they loved best: books like E. Nesbit's *The Enchanted Castle*, Edward Eager's *The Time Garden*, or the battered Roger Lancelyn edition of Robin Hood's adventures.

In her mind's eye, Emily saw those books and more heaped in the hammock where she and Anne had read peacefully that afternoon. Dull red covers and shiny green ones, slim, dog-eared paperbacks, and an immense, illustrated edition of Tolstoy's *War and Peace* that Anne had insisted on checking out despite the librarian's dubious stare. After seeing the movie version with Audrey Hepburn, Anne had danced about in her nightgown for hours pretending to be the heroine, Natasha, at her first ball, until Emily and Will decided enough was enough and bombarded her with pillows. Tickled into submission, she begged for a truce, and as forfeit had to read "Jack and the Beanstalk," Will's favorite story, aloud three times. That, too, lay in the hammock, in the warped, weather-beaten picture-book version that had been their father's. Will had tossed it there before they set off together for the library.

But where, oh where, was the mysterious little book with the illegible title, the enchanted book that had sucked them unawares into this storybook world? It had tumbled into the grass of some distant forest clearing. And without it, they might never get home again.

Emily closed her eyes and shook her head hard, feeling her bangs brush against her forehead.

"Emily Thornton, 634 Newberry Street, 555-0765," she said quickly, her eyes still shut tight. "Hackett Avenue School, 4B. My father is John Thornton, foreign news editor for *The Daily Herald*. My mother is Elizabeth Baumgarten, garden columnist and illustrator. 'Garden with Baumgarten,' Sundays and Wednesdays, in Section Two."

"Poor poppet, 'tis the shock," said old Thomas, the gnarled grandfather who had wanted to strangle Sir Reynold Pomfret. "Give her something to settle her wits. That's it," he added as Emily choked a bit on the sweet wine Marian held to her lips. "Take a good swallow. Now, tell it slow and sensible."

So much for facts, thought Emily. Opening her eyes, she saw Robin's angular face and impatient look, the puzzled expression etched into old Thomas's wrinkles—and, a few feet away, the frightened glance the abbot threw her between his fits of coughing.

Real or not, there was no turning back. Pulling herself together, Emily recounted all she could remember of the exchange between Pomfret and the abbot, though she hadn't understood its meaning.

Marian and Robin glanced at each other, their faces somber.

"The Richard they spoke of is surely the king," Marian said. "We have been awaiting his return from the Crusades these many months. His brother Prince John has all but usurped the throne, and seized the lands of Richard's loyal followers, making outlaws and beggars of England's honest folk."

Robin nodded, looking grim. "Sad news indeed if Richard is taken prisoner," he said, "but sadder still if his evil brother gains time and scope to plot worse against him. I would know more from red-faced abbot, yonder."

It took only a few threats and the sight of a stout cudgel to bring the abbot to a full confession of his conversation with Pomfret. Denying prior knowledge of any plot, he repeated what the dark knight had unveiled to him.

Richard was being held prisoner in a castle in Austria. While the king's capture was still secret, his jailors were prepared to dispose of him quietly and permanently—for a price. Otherwise, they would announce their royal catch and formally demand a ransom for his release. Pomfret, the last link in a relay of messengers from Austria, had been riding hard to put the secret offer in front of Prince John before it expired.

"Treason and treachery," said Robin in the stillness that followed the abbot's words. His voice was quiet, but his eyes flashed anger. "By all that's holy, Reynold Pomfret shall rue the day he thought to betray his sovereign. But thanks to you and your sister, lass, he shall not succeed. Now let all join the search, for the traitor must be caught at all costs, and your sister brought back safe."

Then he clapped Emily on the back, and she felt a thrill of pride.

"I'm coming, too," she declared.

Robin grinned. "Here, take this," he said, and unbuckling a small, sheathed dagger from his belt, he fastened it around her waist. "We'll have you harvesting purses next, milady. Now, look sharp, and not a word till I give the signal."

They fanned out into the forest, Emily right behind Robin and Marian, trying to match their sure-footed stealth in the shadows.

The night was very still now, and every sound seemed magnified. When an owl hooted, Emily stumbled and would have fallen without Robin's steadying hand. Afterwards, her breath seemed noisy to her own ears. They had gone only a hundred feet or so when Marian halted and motioned Robin to stop. To Emily, the forest seemed no different, but Robin ducked down behind a tree and signaled the others to do the same. For what seemed like ages, they waited.

Emily, crouched behind a stand of brambles, grew scratchy and impatient.

What were they waiting for anyway? Did Robin and Marian think Pomfret was just going to waltz right into an ambush? She longed to call out for Anne, who must be lost and alone by now. Poor Anne. Fingering the hilt of her dagger, Emily felt brave and impetuous. How impressed Anne would be, not to mention Robin Hood, if she, Emily Thornton, captured Pomfret single-handed instead of hiding in the bushes.

Patience had never been Emily's virtue. Once, playing hide-and-seek indoors on a rainy Sunday, she had squeezed into a suitcase in the attic, burrowing under old baby clothes, only to abandon her impregnable position out of boredom before Anne had even searched the top floor. Anne caught her as she made a dash for home, which was an overstuffed blue armchair in the living room. Somehow in the process, an ungainly Chinese lamp and spindly-legged end table crashed and splintered. "Not the T'ang Ying lamp!" their father had howled, emerging inconveniently from his study. "How many times have I told you . . ." Will, on the other hand, who made stubbornness a form of patience, was still curled under the kitchen sink around the garbage bin when their mother began peeling potatoes for supper, long after the game had ended in tears and recriminations.

But Emily was not thinking of childish games now. Running a hand through her short, curly brown hair in a way she thought dashing, she narrowed her eyes, clasped the dagger, and began to rise from her uncomfortable crouch. As she did so, she heard a stifled scream from behind an oak tree a few yards ahead, then a scrabbling sound in the leaves and a muffled thud.

"Anne!" she cried, flinging herself through the brambles and sprinting straight for the tree—and straight into the steely grip of Sir Reynold Pomfret.

Too late, much too late, she saw he had Anne gagged and tied behind the oak. Before Emily's dagger was out of its sheath, he had wrestled it from her, and holding her fast with one arm, he set the blade against her throat from behind.

"Oh, Robin Hooood," he called out over her head in a

mocking singsong. " 'Tis said you let no harm come to women and children. If you would save these two blundering fools, bring me my horse at once and give me safe escort to the Nottingham high road."

"Fine knightly manners, Pomfret," Robin replied. "Have you no shame? Loose those children, and face me squarely in equal combat, and if you win, my men will show you on to Nottingham, my word on it."

Pomfret's laugh was like a sneer.

"This is no game, outlaw, and I am no callow youth to catch with chivalrous nonsense. Quick, go for my horse, or I'll begin the carving."

If there hadn't been a knife at her throat, Emily might have hung her head in shame. She caught Anne's eye, and wished she hadn't: the how-could-you-be-so-stupid look was unmistakable. Emily felt her face turn hot with humiliation, then anger.

"You coward," she said, twisting in Pomfret's grasp. "You villainous . . . jerk. You're not going to get away with this."

"Oh, won't I?" He gave her ankle a quick, vicious kick. "Now, keep your mouth shut."

The hours that followed were among the most miserable of Emily's life. Hands tied with her own belt, and ignominiously slung across the horse in front of Pomfret, she felt every bump in the forest floor. Anne, who rode sidesaddle in the arc of the knight's cruel arm, was not much better off.

And when Pomfret's stallion finally emerged from the trees and they saw the Nottingham high road stretching pale and empty in the light of the waning moon, their hearts sank. By Pomfret's order, on pain of their lives, only Will Scarlet, unarmed, had accompanied them to show the way. But they still had hoped for rescue.

"Be of stout heart, lasses," Scarlet called after them. "Robin'll save you yet."

The words gave little comfort in the cold light of dawn, when the jailor of Nottingham castle thrust them roughly into a stone-walled cell, and they heard the dungeon door clang shut behind him.

"Of all the dumb things to do," said Anne, who was finally free of her gag.

"Me? How about you, running off into the woods like that, getting yourself captured. It's all your fault."

It was one of those sordid quarrels that finally end in tears, mumbled apologies, and hugs, but only after many bitter words and a few wounds.

"Let's survey our situation," Anne said at last, after they'd made up. She chewed on the end of her right braid and peered up at the tiny, barred window six feet above their heads. "Maybe it's not so bad."

"You don't even know the worst of it," Emily said miserably.

She told Anne about Pomfret's treachery, and the likelihood that evil Prince John was even now sending gold to King Richard's Austrian captors to purchase his execution.

"They probably want tons of money," Anne said thoughtfully, hugging her knees. The girls had heaped together the thin layer of straw that covered the stone floor and were huddling on it in one corner of the damp cell. "He won't be able to collect it all that fast, I bet. That'll give us time to make a plan."

Emily felt vaguely comforted. After all, they had often played at being prisoners. Aristocratic prisoners in the Tower of London, prisoners of war scaling enemy fortifications, the Count of Monte Cristo digging himself out of the Château d'If. And Anne—who always got to be the count, or the captain, or Princess Elizabeth, just because she was older and knew the stories—Anne always had a plan. For once, instead of feeling resentful, Emily felt so grateful, she fell into an exhausted sleep.

But Anne lay awake, worrying. Like Emily, she had thought back to the moments before they were swept into Pomfret's path, and about the small, nondescript book that had tumbled from their laps when they rose to the sound of hoofbeats.

All magic has its rules, she knew that. But whatever rules, whatever power had brought them to this place and time were contained in that book. And where was it? Lost in the depths of Sherwood Forest. Or worse, lying on the lawn of an old brown-shingled house in Queens where a mother called and called, but no one answered.

NOTTINGHAM CASTLE

$\mathcal{A}$nne and Emily were awakened by the creak of the cell door and the thump of two wooden bowls on the floor.

"Gruel, sweethearts," said the guard. "Eat up. There'll be no more till suppertime, if they let you live that long."

He splashed down cups of water, too, and a hunk of moldy bread. Then he grinned, stretching the pockmarks on his sallow face and wiping his long nose with the back of a grimy hand. Before they could respond, he was gone, the door shut tight behind him.

The gruel was a little like instant oatmeal when you've poured in too much water, Anne thought, staring at the thin, gray stuff. Except sour and disgusting, she decided after tasting it with a shudder. Emily, who had come to the same conclusion, was trying to crumble the moldy spots off the bread.

"It's okay under the green stuff, Anne," she said, trying a chunk.

"Well, at least the water's normal." Anne drained her cup. "Listen, Em, I've got an idea. It's so obvious, I don't know why we didn't think of it before. I mean, this is all magic, right?"

Emily nodded, chewing the stale bread, which tasted particularly unmagical.

"What if we just wish? Hold hands and wish to be home? Maybe it'll work."

They tried, grasping hands at the center of the narrow cell, looking up to the patch of light at the high window and the dark iron bars that broke it.

"Oh, Magic," intoned Anne, "we wish we were home."

Nothing happened. After some whispered consultation, they tried again in unison: "Magic, take us home!"

"Please," added Emily. The grim stone walls remained as solid and forbidding as ever, and in the diffuse light their faces looked even paler.

"That's what I was afraid of," Anne said glumly, kicking at the straw. "The magic's in the book, and, like idiots, we dropped it who knows where."

Emily sat down on the cold floor and turned back to the bread. She was surprised by her own lack of disappointment.

"How can we leave without trying to fix things, anyway?" she asked. "I mean, don't you think we're meant to keep Prince John from having King Richard killed?"

Anne looked at her little sister with a mixture of affection and exasperation. "Good old Em," she said. "And how are we going to do that, cooped up in this smelly dungeon starving to death?"

Just then, they heard voices outside the door, and a key turned in the lock.

"Straight to His Royal Highness," a man with a commanding voice was saying. "And mind they get there without incident. Let's have a look, now."

A portly, ruddy-faced fellow wearing a gold chain and a self-important expression stepped through the door, backed by four men-at-arms. "Not very impressive, I must say," he declared, staring down his nose at Anne and Emily.

"Not very impressive yourself," said Emily rudely. Hunger always made her cross.

"Who are you anyway?" asked Anne, who for once wasn't embarrassed by Emily's outburst.

"Who, indeed," the man huffed, tugging at the gold chain and pawing the medallion that hung there against his russet robe. "I'm the Lord Sheriff of Nottingham, that's who. Take that tone with me again and I shall have you hanged, do you hear? Of course, I may have you hanged anyway."

Anne and Emily exchanged glances.

"I imagined him taller," Emily whispered. "And not so fat. No wonder he never catches Robin Hood."

One of the men-at-arms, a tall youth with the snub-nosed look of an overgrown peasant boy, tried to stifle a giggle. The Sheriff whirled on him, one hand on the hilt of his broadsword. "As for you, you porridge-faced oaf, hold your peace or you'll be back in the pig sty you came from."

"Enough!" came a familiar snarl just outside the open door. It was Pomfret, stamping his freshly polished boots in impatience. "His Highness wants to question them himself, and we have no time to lose. Make them presentable if you can, and bring them to the Great Hall within the quarter hour."

He turned on his heel, the satin lining of his fine black cloak rippling scarlet for a moment as he went. The Sheriff was left to gnaw his mustache and cover his anger with many sharp orders to the men.

"Brush off that straw," he barked. "Not like that, you curs. Well, don't just stand there, clodhoppers, bind their hands. Ha! Small wonder Robin Hood remains at large when I am served by such fools."

The four men-at-arms said nothing, but Anne thought she caught some resentful glances pass among them as they tried to follow the Sheriff's orders, tying the girls' hands behind their backs with rope and brushing the worst of the grubby dungeon straw from their jerkins.

Two in front and two behind, the guards quick-marched Anne and Emily up the steep dungeon steps. Then came more locked doors and gloomy passages that dully echoed the sound of marching feet. Turning up to climb a small, dark staircase, they ran into a frightened scullion, his small, pointed chin all greasy with the roasted chicken leg he'd been eating in secret. He scurried off, leaving a faint smell of onion and drippings behind him.

At the top of the stairs they came to a corridor, and a

wide, arched doorway hung with heavy green velvet. The Sheriff, breathing noisily (for he had been hard-pressed to keep up with his men), ushered in Anne and Emily himself.

The Great Hall was dazzling after the dungeon. Bright tapestries hung on every wall, threaded with scarlet and saffron and spring green. Sunlight winked in the silver goblets that lined the long table, and brass plates glowed on fine white damask. A fire leaped high upon the central hearth, and on the floor the rushes were freshly strewn and smelled of lavender. At the far end of the huge room, on a kind of stage, they saw a man in a fur-trimmed purple robe whose many rings caught the light as he moved his hand to his mouth and away again.

It was Prince John, and he was eating grapes.

"How tiresome," he told the Sheriff, who was bowing and scraping until Emily longed to kick his fat behind. "If such dreary, half-grown peasants are truly bait for Robin of Locksley, why haven't you rid us of him long ago, eh?"

Prince John spat a grape seed in the Sheriff's direction, and reached for the bunch again. He was a smooth-skinned, well-fed man with small, rodentlike features and thinning black hair.

"Leave us, Sheriff," he said in a bored voice, shifting in the heavy, elaborately carved chair that was serving as his throne. "Sir Reynold, think you really to entice the outlaw hither with these, these . . . creatures?"

Emily glared. Anne, too stung to speak, remembered from the reams of English history that she'd absorbed that John, known as John Lackland, was the weak, under-handed brother in an otherwise handsome, robust royal family, and, like many weaklings, a bully. *Creep*, she thought.

But she couldn't help imagining how she and Emily must look to him, scratched and earth-smudged from their forest journey, with bits of dungeon straw sticking in their hair. Seeing their clothes in the light of day for the first time, she found them rough and ungainly. Her hose bagged at the knees, and her feet, shod in brown leather, suddenly looked enormous.

Anne had grown like a weed in the last year—*like a weed*, that was the expression her mother had used, laugh-ing and rumpling her hair, oblivious to how the word hurt. It had been the first warm evening of spring, and her mother, who could be beautiful even in muddy jeans and a gardening smock, was dressed for a party, her curly dark mane brushed to a soft shine about her shoulders, a flow of flowered silk skimming her slim waist and eddying about her ankles. "Oh, darling," she'd said, looking at Anne's at-tempt to dress up for the guests in last year's favorite summer dress. "You've really outgrown it completely. Don't you have something else?"

Then her father, always as nervous before a party as he was calm under newspaper deadlines, bellowed from downstairs about the stuffed mushrooms burning in the broiler, and her mother disappeared to deal with the crisis. Left alone in her parents' bedroom, where her mother's perfume still caressed the air, Anne had studied her reflection in the full-length mirror and hated what she saw: a girl with big feet and skinny legs too long for her body, and awkward elbows that made the puffed sleeves of the pale-blue dress look ridiculous. The bodice was as tight as sausage casing and bunched under the arms, and the hem, let out as far as it would go last August, didn't even reach her skinned knees.

She had drawn closer to the mirror, studying her face and hating every freckle, hating her straight brown hair encased in its two braids, and watching her dark eyes fill with tears.

And then Emily had burst in, small and compact and curly-haired, perfectly adorable in puffed sleeves, jabbering about what fun it would be to spy on the grownups' party from the staircase after they were sent to bed. By the time their mother had returned in search of Anne, carrying a plain school skirt and a silly embroidered blouse that

Grandmother had once sent from Mexico, Anne had locked herself in the bathroom.

The Great Hall of Nottingham Castle was a place for brilliant silk gowns and rich brocades, she thought now, for the sweep and rustle of ladies' skirts and the flourish of feathered caps in candlelight, not for homespun jerkins and sturdy shoes.

Pomfret was striding from one end of the dais to the other, holding his impatience in check with difficulty.

"Your Highness, the outlaw band that yesterday was naught but an annoyance today may stand 'twixt you and England's throne," he said. " 'Tis no small sum, ten thousand ducats, but it can be raised. The loyal barons who feast here today in your honor will see to that, for many a rich storeroom and treasure chest remain in the hands of our Saxon foes, and they are ripe now for the plucking. But with a scurvy outlaw band ruling the roads through Sherwood, no treasure can be safely gathered, nor pass unhindered to the coast."

He paused and smote his fist into his palm.

"Strike now, Your Highness, baiting the trap well first, and such troubles are over. Depend upon it, this Robin Hood is full of himself, giddy with old-fashioned notions of chivalry. By my troth, he fancies himself a chevalier of the legendary Round Table, and will not stand idly by in

Sherwood while we prepare to hang his outlaw cubs."

Prince John sucked on a grape and flicked an imaginary piece of dust from his gold-flocked purple sleeve.

"But how much does he know already?" he asked fretfully. "Enough to spoil it all, perhaps. You said yourself the Abbot of Hereford is a fool and not likely to have held his tongue. I would discover from these outlaw minions what story is now abroad.

"You there," he said in a louder voice, pointing at Anne. "Where is Richard, His Majesty my brother?"

Anne said nothing. Turning her head, she stared out the casement windows. Beyond the town wall, beyond the hedges and hillocks and neatly plowed fields, she could see the dark edges of Sherwood. She was thinking hard.

"Answer His Highness's question, wench," Pomfret demanded.

Anne looked him squarely in the face. "Everyone knows that Richard the Lion-Hearted was taken prisoner in Austria on his way back from the Crusades," she said slowly, ignoring Emily's horrified gasp. "Ask anybody. It's not a secret. The ransom is already half collected by now."

Prince John made an exasperated noise, spraying grape seeds in all directions. "Well, there you have it, sirrah. Even worse than I feared. In what ill-timed plot would you embroil me?"

Pomfret clenched his hands, and the scar on his upper lip twitched.

"Lies," he whispered hoarsely. "The story can have gone no further than the outlaws. Let it die on the gallows with them!"

As he spoke, the velvet hanging was thrust aside and the Sheriff, looking pleased with himself, swept back in.

"We've captured another one," he announced. "Notorious fellow called Scarlet. Spreading treasonous gossip in the Blue Boar Tavern and asking for news of these two."

"Gossip? What sort of gossip?" Pomfret's tone was so ominous that the Sheriff's plump face sagged like badly kneaded dough. He sputtered something about a tale of King Richard being held for ransom, then trailed off into nervous silence when Pomfret swore.

Prince John's peevish look turned shrewd, and he stroked his small black goatee.

"Hmm. A foul outlaw scheme to trick money out of the King's loyal subjects, no doubt. Sheriff, let us hang this Scarlet at the town gates at sundown this very day, and these two with him, and let it be widely known that the same fate awaits any man, woman, or child who spreads this false story of the King's capture."

Emily had been shocked when Anne spoke of King Richard's imprisonment, because her instinct was to tell

Prince John nothing, especially not a piece of information that was still largely secret. Now she realized Anne had hoped to force an end to Pomfret's plot, which depended on general ignorance of Richard's capture. Instead, it seemed, she might as well have signed their death warrant, and poor Will Scarlet's, too.

So why was Anne looking so uplifted? Emily caught her eye and saw the unmistakable glow of new confidence.

The Sheriff, pink with pleasure, was bowing and scraping again.

"Certainly, Your Highness. Exactly as you say, Your Highness. Would you prefer them hanged all together, or one after the other, Your Highness?"

Under cover of this gruesome discussion of the fine points, which Prince John seemed to relish, Anne whispered something out of the corner of her mouth.

"Will Scarlet's rescue, Em, remember? The palmer."

And then Emily did remember. It was one of Anne's favorite chapters in their small paperback edition of Robin Hood stories. She had read most of it aloud to Emily one afternoon when Emily had the flu and their mother was doubled over the typewriter trying to write the column on garden mulches that her editor, a tidy, chopped-bark and straight-rows sort of man, insisted on every year.

"I'd like to mulch *him*," Elizabeth Baumgarten had muttered, banging the typewriter carriage. (For that is what writers did for many years before computers were invented.) The clatter of the keys and the ring-slam at the end of each line had been a distant counterpoint to Anne's voice reading the tale of Will Scarlet's rescue.

As Emily remembered the story, Scarlet went to a tavern in disguise, but was seized and recognized when the Sheriff's men raided the place. He was ordered hanged at the town gate, but when the time came, the hangman could not be found, because some of Robin's men had seen to it that he was in a drunken stupor. So the Sheriff asked the large crowd for volunteers, and an old palmer—that was some kind of pilgrim in tattered robes and a broad-brimmed hat—volunteered to hang Scarlet, claiming to have a grudge against him. But when he reached the gallows, he slit the ropes binding Scarlet's hands instead, handed him a broadsword that had been hidden in the folds of his palmer's robe, and drew one himself.

Ta-da! He was really Robin Hood, and the crowd watching the hanging was full of his followers. There was a terrific battle scene, and of course the outlaws won, routing the Sheriff's men and melting back into the forest, with Will Scarlet at their side. Anne had read it wonderfully, using a cackly old voice for the palmer until he turned into Robin Hood, and slapping the side of the rocking chair for emphasis when the outlaws let fly their arrows.

So *that* was the story they had stumbled into! Once, when she was much younger, Emily had wandered away from home, lured on by the tinkling tune of a distant ice cream truck until she suddenly realized she was lost. Just when she was ready to sit down on the curb and howl, she had glimpsed the familiar branches of a gnarled tree hanging over the back fence of an anonymous house. It was a tree in the back corner of her own yard, viewed from around the block. She felt the same flood of relief now.

The wooden door at the far side of the hall swung open, and the room began to bustle with the scurrying of pages and serving maids. Some carried garlands of woodruff and forget-me-nots to decorate the tables. Others bore big pitchers of beaten silver and waxen candles, tall in their fluted holders. Each time the door opened, the rich scent of roasting meat wafted in from the kitchen below.

Prince John watched the preparations with satisfaction.

"Nothing like a sunset hanging to entertain one's guests after a midday feast, I must say. What good fortune to have captured this Scarlet fellow, a big, bold knave from what I've heard, who'll make a fine display at the end of a rope. 'Twould have been but a poor show, Sheriff, with only these two pipsqueaks to hang."

This was too much for Emily.

"Pipsqueaks, huh?" she said, flushing. "You think you're pretty clever, don't you, Your High and Mightiness. Well, you're not half as clever as Robin Hood. I can't wait to see your face when he throws off his old palmer disguise and rescues Will Scarlet. And by the way, King Richard does get ransomed in the end, and comes home and punishes all those bad barons and pardons Robin Hood and you have to beg his forgiveness and slink away in disgrace. So there!"

Too late, Emily saw the glitter in Pomfret's eyes, the prince's penetrating stare, and her sister's horrified face.

"Old palmer disguise, eh?" said Pomfret, drawing close to her. "Well, well, well. Prattle on, pipsqueak prophetess. What other tricks has the outlaw rogue in store?"

"She was kidding," Anne said desperately. "You know, speaking in jest. She's only a little girl. She doesn't really know anything."

"We'll see about that," snapped Pomfret. "Sheriff, lock them in the northwest chamber. I shall question them both further at my leisure. Clearly they are too useful to hang—yet."

Prince John gave a tight-lipped smile and a dismissive wave of the hand.

"They can be hanged in the next batch, with Robin Hood. Sheriff, alert your men to watch for an old palmer. Even you can't bungle his capture this time."

※

It was much to Anne's credit that after they heard the door slam and the key turn in the lock and the Sheriff's footsteps retreat into silence she did not turn on Emily and ask, "How could you?" But to Emily, her sister's silence was worse than all the angry reproaches in the world. Guilt-stricken and scared, she supplied the words herself.

"How could I be so stupid? Oh, Anne, I've ruined everything."

"Yes," her sister said bleakly.

They were seated awkwardly on a large wooden chest near the only window in the room. It was a sparsely furnished chamber, but rather grand, with hangings of red cloth draped around the bed, a long table of polished walnut, and heavy iron torch holders protruding from the walls; a spare-bedroom kind of place, really, but a definite improvement on the dungeon cell, at least until Pomfret, "at his leisure," decided to interrogate them.

"I just don't understand how this works," Emily went on. "Is the whole story going to be changed now because of me? Like, instead of "The Rescue of Will Scarlet," it'll be "The Capture of Robin Hood"?

"I don't know," Anne said wearily. "There are lots of different versions of the Robin Hood stories. In the Howard Pyle book that I got from the library one time it wasn't even Will Scarlet who had to be rescued. It was a character called Will Stutely, or Will-the-Bowman. The stories come from a lot of different old ballads, handed down through the years." Her voice grew bitter. "Who knows? Maybe there always *was* a version where somebody betrayed Robin Hood and he got caught. Or maybe there only will be now."

The word *betrayed* could have pushed Emily over the edge into tears of despair. Instead it stung her into action. She rose from the chest and turned to face Anne.

"We have to escape, that's all there is to it. We have to warn Robin before he falls into the trap."

"And how do you propose to do that?" asked Anne in an unforgiving tone.

Emily looked wildly around the room.

"The bedsheets!" she exclaimed. "We could tie them together and climb out the window."

"Well," retorted her sister, "aside from the fact that our hands are tied and that we'd probably break our necks, that's a brilliant idea."

Ignoring Anne's sarcasm, Emily craned her neck to

see out the window. It was a sheer drop fifty feet to the cobblestone courtyard, and she could see the glint of armor below. They were directly above the castle guard's drill yard.

"Drat. Oh, well, there's got to be another way. Come on, Anne. Don't just sit there. Let's find something to cut through these ropes."

She walked across the room to the table. There wasn't much on it. A candlestick, unlit, of course. An earthenware jug filled with water. A small mirror with an ivory handle. The mirror? No, the jug, Emily thought. If they could smash it on the table, she was sure she could hold a sharp, broken piece against the rope binding Anne's wrists and saw through it.

The job was harder than she'd thought, and messier. Water doused them both, and tiny bits of shattered pottery flew everywhere, while the bigger pieces slithered away from her grasp in the puddle on the table. But at last, with much grunting and quarreling and a few cuts on both sides, Anne's hands were free, and her own were soon afterwards.

But after trying the heavy door, looking out the window once more, even checking the sooty fireplace for a possible roofward exit, they found they were as imprisoned as ever.

By now they could hear strains of music from the Great Hall, as well as footsteps and voices of guests gathering for the feast. They hoped the dinner would keep Pomfret occupied for a while, but every time they heard a footfall, they feared he had come to question them. And though the sun was still high in the sky, it was edging westward, relentlessly moving toward its rendezvous with the horizon, and Will Scarlet's rendezvous with the gallows.

They sat down on the chest again, discouraged. Anne looked at Emily's damp cloth jerkin and at her own, the Lincoln green blackened by cinders and stained with blood from the rope-cutting struggle.

"I wish we could change," she muttered absently, though the state of their clothing was surely the least of their worries.

But Emily was staring back at her with dawning excitement.

"The chest!" she whispered. "I have a great idea . . ."

It wasn't locked.

The heavy lid swung silently on oiled hinges, revealing a deep pile of velvets, shimmering silks, and rich brocades. There were cloaks and robes and doublets of every hue, feathered caps and embroidered slippers and soft leather belts clasped with silver. Here was a small plum-

colored cape lined in saffron yellow, and a saffron doublet
with purple hose to match, just Emily's size. There was a
sapphire-blue robe with pointed sleeves and gold brocade
at every hem—no, it was too big. But yes, here was a
wine-red gown that could have been seamstress-fitted for
Anne, a slim-waisted gown with a long, graceful skirt that
skimmed the floor, and flowing sleeves, opening like bell-
flowers to show their silver silk lining.

"Oh, Anne, you're beautiful," breathed Emily when
her sister had slipped the dress on, unfastening her braids
so her dark hair fell in ripples against the crimson silk.
And tilting the hand mirror in the afternoon light, Anne
could see that it was so.

But there was no time to waste in admiration. This
was no ordinary game of dress-up. And when they
climbed into the chest and pulled the lid shut, after dangling twined bedsheets out the open window, they both
knew they were playing hide-and-seek for their lives.

ESCAPE

$\mathcal{T}$he feast was in full swing when the pale-faced messenger thrust his way through the tumult of guests, minstrels, and jesters, past shiny-faced servants still hoisting huge platters of roast peacock and suckling pig from the kitchen, past the snuffling hunting hounds who nosed for bones among the rushes, and up to the high table.

He whispered something to the Sheriff of Nottingham, and the Sheriff's florid face turned a bilious green. The Sheriff stood up and seemed to totter, casting a baleful glance at Pomfret, who was several feet away in a place of honor and did not notice.

"It cannot be," the Sheriff muttered, clutching the ring of keys at his waist. "I shall come at once."

Back through the crowd they went together, the Sheriff and the messenger, down the corridor to the northwest chamber door, where half a dozen guards stood waiting. With trembling fingers, the Sheriff turned the heavy key in the lock and pushed.

Immediately his eye took in the empty room, the open window, and the bedsheets, twisted into a rope and tied to an iron torch holder, dangling down to freedom.

"They've escaped!" he cried, aghast. A sudden vision of Pomfret's fury and Prince John's contempt made him weak, and he collapsed against the bed frame. "After them, you fools!" he shrieked. "Down to the courtyard! Search the stables! Sound the alarm! Quick, quick!"

The guards rushed from the room, and the Sheriff panted after them. They clattered down the stairs and out to the drill yard, and then ran frantically between barracks and stables, searching in vain for two striplings in Lincoln green.

The Sheriff, of course, was far too busy and far too distraught to think of locking the northwest chamber door behind him. And so the pretty, dark-haired young lady in crimson silk and her charming little page in purple velvet slipped ever so easily out into the corridor a few seconds later. They melted unnoticed into the gaily clad throng in the Great Hall.

A round-faced serving maid seated them without question just in time for the sweetmeats. Candied figs and apricots, rich lemon tarts, and raspberry syllabub were set before them. As they took their bearings, they ate, licking their sticky fingers over the first food they'd had that day since dungeon gruel and moldy bread.

They were among yeomen and burghers at the back of the room, and from that safe distance they could observe the high table, thick with barons and courtiers. Pomfret was still there, his head bent in conversation with a bearded knight on his right. But once the Sheriff returned to confess his prisoners' disappearance, Pomfret would un-doubtedly take charge of the search himself. Unlike the bumbling Sheriff, he would be shrewd enough to look in the chest. And there, crumpled at the bottom, he would find their suits of Lincoln green.

There was no time to lose.

Still, they mustn't draw attention to themselves. Even if they could leave now without arousing notice, which way would they turn when they left the Great Hall? Not knowing the castle, they might easily end up face-to-face with the Sheriff and his men.

They saw the velvet hangings stir, and a dark-haired lady slipped into the hall. Her dress was of grass-green silk, and it seemed to float over the rushes as she stepped past the high table. Now she was sweeping a fine, low curtsy, her long skirt falling in gleaming folds around her, her back so straight and supple that she radiated quiet pride, not humility. Anne couldn't take her eyes away.

"Lady Marian Fitzwater," one of the burghers at their table whispered to another. "And lovely as ever, for all they say she is brokenhearted over the banishment of Robin of Locksley."

Of course, it was Marian—Marian, who was as fleet-footed and quick-witted as the best of Robin's companions in the greenwood, where she was perfectly capable of am-bushing an abbot or disarming a knight. But here in the banquet hall, she was also in her element. Graceful and serene, she knew how to glide between both worlds.

Scullions and serving maids cleared the sweetmeat platters and disappeared through a door at the back. They returned with bowls of rose-scented water and linen tow-els for hand washing. In the musicians' gallery above, the music quickened into the lively measures of a dance, and a jester, his clothes a tattered, piebald mix of fantastic colors, leaped upon a table.

Nimbly, he danced among the wine goblets and fingerbowls, and so lightly that not a drop was spilled. To the crowd's delight, after giving a bow and a flourish of his belled cap to Prince John, he drew five glittering balls of silver filigree from a red leather bag at his side and, tossing them up, began to juggle. High and higher they went, sparkling as they tumbled, only to be caught and sent spinning up again.

"Now," someone said softly, "follow me, and quickly."

It was Marian, just behind them. Quietly they rose from the table, and quickly, quickly, she took them to the door that led to the kitchen steps. There stood a minstrel in strange black-and-silver garb.

The broad, red-feathered cap he wore was cocked so low upon his brow that it shadowed his face, and he held a lute, as though waiting to perform. But at his side gleamed a broadsword. Anne recognized him first. Something about the lean, angular jawline under the foppish cap, the set of the broad shoulders, the twinkle just visible in his shadowed eyes: it was Robin Hood, and he was smiling.

"Well met," whispered Marian, touching his hand before she slipped back into the crowd.

Down the stairs Anne and Emily ducked after Robin, into the great steamy kitchens. Sweating scullions were scraping roasted meat off bones, piling greasy platters and trenchers high, and hauling great tubs of water to the hot bricks of the hearth. An immense aproned woman stood in their path, sleeves rolled and fat, rosy arms sternly folded across her ample bosom.

"Have you lost your manners, young Robin?" she asked. "A fine way to trample through a woman's kitchen."

But Robin laughed and kissed her plump, pink cheek, and she embraced him.

"Ah, Tilda," he said. "Many's the time my mouth's watered for the currant buns you used to bake at Locksley Chase."

"I'd bake 'em, and you'd filch 'em," retorted the cook, flushing even rosier, unable to keep the pleased smile from her lips. "Get along with you now, out the kitchen garden gate and follow the stream through the hedge. You'll soon be back in the greenwood then."

They were hardly through the door when she ran after them, out of breath, with a bulging sack in her hands and three plain brown cloaks over her arm.

"Currant buns," she said. "Good honey cake, enough for the lot of you. And something to hide those popinjay trappings. Faith, that scarlet hat makes a target of you from Barnsdale to Dinsmore, and the young'uns' gaudy colors, all the more. Now, off with you!"

＊

The sun was slanting golden through the trees by the time the three dodged into the cool forest. Robin had tossed his red-feathered hat into the shining brook, and looking back, Anne could still see it, tiny in the distance, bobbing and spinning downstream.

"Robin," she panted, "they're going to hang Will Scarlet at sundown."

"So they think, pretty maid," he replied, "but fear not. 'Tis not so easy to hang one of mine." Cupping his hands to his mouth, he gave the outlaw's call, and before long, two dozen men appeared to do his bidding. They were dressed not in green but in leather jerkins of homespun brown, and a few in fine cloaks like those worn by townspeople.

"How now, Diccon," Robin asked one, "is the hangman well along in his cups?"

"Aye, master," said Diccon, who was cousin to the potboy at the Golden Stag Tavern. "Isaac was filling his tankard to the brim again when I left them, and the old devil could barely sit straight enough to drink it."

"And have you the clothes, Roger?" Robin asked.

"Here they be," declared a sturdy, brown-faced man, holding out a broad-brimmed palmer's hat in one hand, and a voluminous robe such as a palmer would wear in the other.

Anne elbowed Emily. Emily stared at the forest floor, sick at heart.

"No, Robin," she said in a small, choked voice that brought a hush to the group. "No, the old palmer trick won't work."

"And why not?" asked Robin lightly, but with a grave look in his eyes.

"It won't work because they're expecting it. And they're expecting it because . . . because I told them about it."

There was a murmur of dismay from the men, and as Emily stuttered apologies, Anne broke in, trying to explain that it had been an accident, a mistake, and all because of a story called "The Rescue of Will Scarlet."

"You see, where we come from it's already in a book," she pressed on, her voice too loud as the men fell silent again.

"I like it not," spoke up Roger, his honest voice heavy with suspicion. "This talk of books that tell of things not past—smacks of witchcraft, I say."

But Robin put a reassuring hand on Anne's shoulder and laughed.

"Tales to frighten babes," he said. "If it's a palmer they expect, we must give them something else, methinks." He turned back to Anne. "Is there not some other trick in this book of which you speak, one still unbeknownst to yonder Sheriff?"

"Well," answered Anne, considering carefully, "not a really useful one, I'm afraid."

But Emily had seen a chance to redeem herself.

"Anne, remember *The Scarlet Pimpernel?*" she said in a rush. "After we saw the old black-and-white movie with Leslie Howard, remember you found the book by that baroness. The rescue from the guillotine!"

Anne's face lit up.

"Yes," she agreed. "That's right. I checked out the book again yesterday—or whenever that was. It's probably still lying in the hammock back home."

She turned to meet Robin's quizzical stare and began to talk in earnest.

"See, there's this family that's going to be executed, and the Scarlet Pimpernel and his band have to rescue them. And so he disguises himself . . ."

✳

Two hours later, when the shadows fell long and thin across the fields and the sun was turning red in its descent, a clatter of men-at-arms filled the narrow streets of Nottingham town. In their midst, a tall, bearded man stood bareheaded in an open cart. His hands were tied, but he looked proudly straight ahead as the crowd surged and muttered around him, some lamenting his fate.

"A good man, Will Scarlet," cried one old man, leaning on a knotty staff. "He fed many a starving family, though it was with the King's deer. Woe is me that I should see him hang."

But many had gathered to see Will Scarlet hanged. Gaily clad castle guests mixed with more somber townspeople, and rough fellows tumbled out of taverns to join the throng. There was a press of yeomen returning from market day to their farms, too, this one with a cart full of barrels, that one driving a gaggle of geese, another one leading a reluctant donkey harnessed to a wagon stacked with pots and pans.

The Sheriff of Nottingham, still chewing his lower lip over the disappearance of his two young prisoners, kept peering into the flow of people from his perch on a fine brown palfrey, anxiously searching for an old palmer with Robin Hood's face. His men were so intent on the same task that again and again they let the jostling crowd push close against them, nearly stopping the procession, before they drove them off again with glancing blows and cries of "Back, back" and "Give way!"

Finally, in this halting style, they reached the main

gate in the town wall. On the other side stood the gallows in the center of a small, grassy square, and a throng of people had gathered there, mostly from neighboring farms and villages. Sir Reynold Pomfret and two score of Prince John's men-at-arms waited with them, also scanning the crowd for a palmer, and uneasily eyeing the darkening mass of Sherwood Forest in the distance.

Suddenly the bugle sounded for the gate to be opened, and the crowd pressed close once more. The youth driving the geese tripped and fell near the Sheriff's horsemen. The geese ran squawking under the mounts, beating their wings and spooking the horses, who shied and kicked. The reluctant donkey chose this moment to break into a run, sending pots and pans flying, and only halted when his cart became wedged tight between two other wagons, one piled with hay, the other loaded with wooden barrels, all blocking the path to the gate. The bent old woman driving the hay wagon began to curse in a high, cracked voice, hitting her whip against the side of the donkey cart, which only made the pots rattle louder.

Suddenly a shout from one of the armed horsemen broke through the din and confusion: "A palmer! There, in the doorway!"

And rising in his stirrups, the Sheriff screamed, "Catch him, catch him!"

The crowd swayed and broke as the mounted men wheeled their frightened horses around and surged toward a thin, gray-bearded palmer cringing against the door of a butcher shop.

"There's another one," cried someone else, pointing toward a stoop-shouldered, plump-bellied fellow on the other side of the street, also wearing pilgrim's clothes and clutching his rosary beads. The foot guards, urged on by the Sheriff, tried to push through the hostile crowd to reach him.

One moment the whole tangled mass was stalled, and Will Scarlet's cart was surrounded by armed guards at every flank. The next moment the crowd and the wagons had closed around Scarlet, filling the space left by the guards as they hurled themselves right and left after the palmers.

One moment Scarlet stood in the cart, his hands bound tightly behind him, his heart sinking at the sight of the gallows, which stood framed by the darkness of the arched gateway through the thick town walls. The next moment the cart was propelled through the gate, and the shadow of the arch fell upon Scarlet. He felt the cart rock as an unfamiliar figure leaped from a hay wagon down beside him. It was the figure of a bent old woman, who sliced the ropes that bound his hands.

Seconds later, when the cart emerged from the shadowed archway into the brilliance of the gallows square, the rays of the setting sun glinted on a broadsword in Will Scarlet's hand, and the figure standing shoulder to shoulder with him was no longer an old woman but Robin Hood. And Robin Hood was notching an arrow to his bent bow.

All was confusion in the grassy square, for a similar scene had been played outside the town walls. Just after the bugle had sounded to open the gate, a tall, broad-shouldered man in palmer's clothes had been spotted on the outskirts of the crowd, and Pomfret's men had lurched after him into the press of people. There were angry exclamations from the common folk, and some cursed the Sheriff and Prince John. The prince and his favored guests could be seen quite close by, peering down on the gallows from a parapet lodged between the castle's lowest battlements and the crenellated top of the town wall.

"*Tyrants* to the gallows," called out one woman fiercely, loud enough for Prince John and his rich guests to hear. "Not stouthearted men that follow Robin Hood. Not pilgrims from the Holy Land."

There were cries of agreement, and of "Long live Robin Hood." And when the cart burst from the gate, and the people realized what was afoot, the joyful shout arose, "A rescue, a rescue!"

From the hay in the wagon sprang men in Lincoln green, each with a bow bent and an arrow fitted to the string, taking aim at Pomfret and his men. From the barrels in the barrel wagon jumped more of the same, aiming the other way, at the Sheriff and his troops.

The Sheriff and Pomfret tried to rally their men and to slash their way back to the cart to capture the outlaws. But at every step they were challenged. The crowd now proved to hold many followers of Robin Hood who threw off their hoods and cloaks and drew their swords to meet steel with steel.

The youth who had seemed to have such trouble controlling his geese proved to be nimbler with a rapier, for it was none other than Marian, who had learned her swordsmanship from Robin himself. The big fellow with the recalcitrant donkey—Little John, as it turned out—pulled out a buckler and broadsword from among the pots and skewered half a dozen of the Sheriff's men like so many roasted capons as they came through the gate. He had help from two boys—tinkers' apprentices from the looks of them—who scrambled atop the mound of cookware, seized up frying pans, and bashed every chain-mailed head that came through.

"A double," called the smaller one (whose grin looked a lot like Emily's), bopping two guards in quick succession and watching them stagger toward Little John's flashing broadsword.

"Ha, a home run," exulted the taller one in Anne's voice, as a mustachioed captain dropped his sword and collapsed in a heap, felled by a swing of an iron skillet that would not have disgraced Babe Ruth. "You know, I kind of wish our Will were here to take a turn at bat."

Emily could just see their little brother, fair hair sticking out from his backwards Yankees cap, the tip of his pink tongue showing between determined lips, sturdy grass-stained legs planted wide. "Outta the park!" he would say when his bat connected with the ball, trying to act nonchalant, but flushed with pride. His equal passions for baseball and bugs sometimes created a conflict in the outfield, but never at bat.

"Outta the park," Emily echoed, flourishing her skillet, as another guard bit the dust.

But out in the grassy square near the gallows, some of Robin's men were hard-pressed by Pomfret's troops.

"Diccon, Marian, Little John," called Alan-a-Dale, fighting off four ruffians. Blood dripped from a wound in his left arm.

With a roar, Little John answered the summons so fiercely that many of the guards turned tail and ran back to the shelter of the town walls, spurred on their way by a hail of arrows from the barrel wagon.

"Come back!" screamed the Sheriff, who suddenly found himself and his nervous horse surrounded by outlaws in the grassy square. Quivering with fear and rage, he appealed to the crowd.

"One hundred ducats to the man who takes that varlet Robin Hood," he cried, pointing at Robin.

For answer, Robin let fly an arrow that lifted the Sheriff's hat and revealed his balding head.

"The next shall be two inches lower," he cried, and the crowd roared with laughter as the fat Sheriff fled.

"Straight out of the story," Anne said with glee to Emily as they ran to join the band, regrouping now for a retreat into Sherwood.

"But that isn't," gasped Emily, clutching her sister's sleeve as she saw Pomfret, eyes ablaze, lead a fresh charge that threatened to drive the outlaws back to the town walls.

The dark knight leaned from the saddle as he brought his broadsword whistling down on Robin. Emily hid her eyes.

"Don't worry, it's okay," her older sister said. And sure enough, Robin had ducked, parrying the blow with such skill that Pomfret was unhorsed.

Now the two men were locked in single combat, steel flashing red on steel as the sun sank amid the trees of Sherwood. But it seemed that Pomfret was gaining the upper hand, driving Robin backwards, thrust by thrust and parry by parry, to the very steps of the gallows.

"Up where you belong, outlaw," Pomfret sneered, his breath rasping now, but his eyes triumphant.

And backwards, up the steps, Robin fought on, his face impassive in the fading light.

For a moment, silhouetted by the sunset, they drew close together under the hanging noose, blade locked against blade. Then Robin laughed in Pomfret's face and disengaged, and in one swift movement his sword darted under the dark knight's guard, pierced his right arm, and sent Pomfret's sword flying.

Seeing their leader disarmed and wounded, Pomfret's remaining men scrambled for the safety of the town.

"Now, sir knight," said Robin, his sword at Pomfret's throat, and his voice ringing out over the crowd. "Since I've troubled to get you up to this fine perch, I would not have it go to waste. 'Tis a fine platform for a speech, a speech that tells the truth of King Richard's whereabouts, his capture by a foreign power, and your foul plot to buy his murder."

There were shocked murmurs and cries of anger from the multitude.

"Hang him!" someone shouted.

"Indeed, hanging's the other possibility," rejoined Robin, as sweat coursed down Pomfret's face and his eyes darted a sickened glance at the dangling noose. "But perhaps you'd prefer to entreat your friends to contribute to good King Richard's ransom. Look up—no, not at the noose, man, at the battlements. They're all waiting."

For Prince John and his bejeweled courtiers were still watching helplessly from the ramparts. Prince John, knowing the game was up and seeing the mood of the crowd, chose to put the best face on this turn of events.

In a hollow voice he called out, "We have just received word that my brother the King is held captive in Austria, and we are collecting a ransom for his safe release."

"Are you, indeed, Your Highness," Robin challenged him. "Well, well, we shall be only too pleased to assist you."

And with Pomfret still at sword's point, he had the barons on the ramparts throw down their jewels and purses to the ground below. Anne and Emily scrambled to help pluck ruby rings and gold chains from the grass, and fat, chinking money bags that the barons had thought would buy the King's death, not his freedom.

"For Richard Lion-Heart," shouted a small, stained tanner in the crowd, tossing a fistful of shillings. And as the crowd cheered, many other loyal subjects followed suit with the coins they could spare. It all went into a great sack that Little John hoisted on his back, promising to see it delivered to Sir Geoffrey Trease, the King's close friend and companion-in-arms, who had returned lately from the Crusades himself and could be trusted to deal properly with Richard's captors.

Then Robin sprang from the gallows and sounded his horn, a long, plaintive note that hovered in the dusk, calling his band back to Sherwood Forest. To those who watched, the outlaws seemed to melt into the landscape like shadows in the night.

To Anne and Emily it was a little more arduous, for they had to scramble to keep up with a pace set by Little John's long strides and Will Scarlet's bounding, joyful lope from field to forest. Scarlet kept drawing deep breaths of the cool evening air, exulting in the life he'd come so close to losing. And Marian, who had looked so proud in silk in the banquet hall, ran easily among the men in her gooseherd's clothes, letting her long dark hair stream in the breeze.

Later, in the firelight of the camp, they all celebrated the rescue with another feast. Robin raised his tankard high to toast Anne and Emily's part in it.

"Very generous, considering," Anne murmured.

But Emily wasn't listening. Alan-a-Dale, his wounded

arm dressed and bandaged by Maid Marian, was cradling his lute a little awkwardly and composing a new ballad for the occasion. The tune he strummed was an old one that Anne and Emily's mother used to sing to them when they were little, after they were tucked in bed for the night, still damp from their baths and wiggling their toes in their footed pajamas. A great yearning for home rose up in them both, and they thought of the book, lying lost in the forest, the pages turning, perhaps, in the Sherwood wind.

"Will, could you take us back to the place where you found us?" Anne asked Scarlet suddenly.

"To the ends of the earth, lass, an' you ask me," he said, still buoyant in the knowledge that he was free to roam after the deer when he wished, and that when he slept he would wake to birdsong.

He lifted them to the warm back of a brown mare, and they set out. They followed a different path this time, shorter and more direct. Or did it only seem that way because of the familiar tune that Scarlet whistled under his breath all the way?

"You know the forest like a book," Anne said in admiration when they halted at the edge of a small clearing.

"Like a book?" asked Scarlet, helping them down. "Nay, like the palm of my own hand."

And stooping, he plucked a small, worn volume

from the grass where it had tumbled, open to the forest floor.

Eagerly, they took it from him, closing the pages between the faded covers.

✳

"A-anne . . . Emileee," came their mother's voice over the hollyhocks. "Suppertime! Come set the table."

They were sitting side by side in the hammock at dusk, a strange little book held closed between them, their own garden hill darkening down to the pine trees, and their own brown house set aglow like a lantern as their mother turned on the lights.

Later that night, scrunched together under the covers of Emily's bed with a flashlight, they read and relived their own adventure. But the remaining pages—two-thirds of the book, at least—would not turn.

"It's like they're stuck together," said Emily, dropping the flashlight in her efforts.

"We still don't know the rules," said Anne. "Maybe we can have another adventure every third day, like in *Magic by the Lake*. Or maybe it'll just take us by surprise. Oh, Em, this is going to be a wonderful summer!"

"But Anne, it's a library book," protested Emily. "We're going to have to return it."

"When's it due?" her sister asked anxiously. They fumbled together for a moment, scrabbling back the pages of the book to the inside front cover.

The words were stamped in the upper-left-hand corner, in the familiar purple ink of the Queens Public Library.

"Date Due: Not Yet."

And with that, they were satisfied, and fell asleep.

WILL'S TURN

Will Thornton woke to the sound of his mother singing in the garden. He lay perfectly still in bed for a moment, watching a patch of sunlight on the wall and listening to the words that reached his open window.

True Thomas lay on Huntlie bank,
And soon a marvel he did see

For there he spied a lady bright
Come riding down by the hawthorne tree.

Her skirt was of the grass-green silk,
Her mantle of the velvet fine;
On every tuft of her horse's mane
Hung fifty silver bells and nine.

His mother was weeding the herb patch just outside the kitchen door, untangling snake grass and clover from the big tufts of thyme and lavender, pulling up the mint sprigs that sprang up unwanted among the parsley, and snipping purple chive blooms so the oniony spears wouldn't go to seed. The air was pungent with the smell of bruised leaves.

It was the middle of July. At seven in the morning, the summer sun was already warm on the pile of books next to Will's bed. They were mostly picture books— "baby books," Emily had called them once in a fit of temper, and Will had flailed at her with his fists in fury. But there was also volume 6 of *Compton's Encyclopedia*, open to the color illustrations of dogs of every breed, which Will was happy to study and compare for hours.

(He remained undecided between wanting an Australian terrier or a Welsh corgi—which was just as well, since his parents refused to get him a dog of any kind. "They dig up flower beds," said his mother, who had been known to talk coaxingly to sick rhododendrons. "They pee on newspapers," said his father, who believed in saving every paper he hadn't had time to read yet.)

Almost hidden under the bed, near the beat-up baseball mitt that had been his uncle Paul's, lay Will's favorite insect book, a pocket-sized paperback with glossy pages and awesome close-ups of such creatures as the praying mantis, Japanese beetle, and tiger-winged moth. "Grotesque," Anne had said with disdain, refusing to have anything to do with the book when Will's best friend, Aaron, gave it to him as a birthday present. But his father had been willing to read it aloud again and again, until Will knew even the Latin names by heart.

Will loved books, but he still couldn't read. He liked the heft and shape of books in his hands, the feel of the pages taut against his thumb as he riffled through them, seeking a favorite illustration. He loved the smell of books, the mustiness of old ones and the stiff, shiny smell of new ones. Sometimes he buried his nose in the binding and breathed deeply, as though to inhale the book instead of reading it. And, in fact, he wished he could.

For trying to decipher even the simple text of his first-grade reader had brought him nothing but frustration. It was as though there were too many letters, too many mixed-up alphabets. He got lost in the forest of big black consonants, waylaid by vowels whose differences were as obvious as the differences between oak and spruce trees, but no more useful to Will in finding a path through the thick woods of a paragraph.

He would be seven in September. At that age Anne and Emily could already read chapter books, while he wouldn't even be able to unravel the boring sentences of a second-grade reader.

"Don't worry," his mother had told him. "It'll just click one of these days and then you'll be able to read anything and everything."

He listened to her singing again, the words muffled because she was bent over the herbs under her broad-brimmed gardening hat. He recognized the song as one of his mother's favorite ballads, *Thomas the Rhymer*, about the poet who was spirited away by the Queen of Elfland.

"Now you must go with me," she said,
"True Thomas, you must go with me,
And you must serve me seven years
Through weal or woe, as chance to be."

"But Thomas, you must hold your tongue
Whatever you may hear or see,
For if you speak word in Elfyn land
You'll never get back to your own country."

All at once he sprang out of bed, sending baseball cards scattering from the folds of his sheet where they seemed to nest, no matter how often he picked up his room. He ran to the window and leaned over the sill, pressing his face against the screen.

The garden stretched out before him, still sparkly with dew. From his second-story vantage point he could see all the landmarks of its terrain: the overhanging branches of the copper beech close by him on the left, between the house and the garage; the little round goldfish pond on the right side of the hill, where flower beds and a stately hedge defined the garden's most formal section; the tangle of raspberry bushes, half hidden by a lilac tree, that sprawled at the farther reaches of the right border; the "secret passage" on the left, running down the hill between the garage and a row of overgrown shrubs that together hid the compost heap from view; the wisteria arbor where the hill sloped flat, its cool gray flagstone floor no longer smothered in pale petals, but shadowed by a leafy canopy; the old apple tree, where a tire swing hung motionless in the morning haze. Finally, the tall pines, guardians of the grassy plain at the bottom of the hill.

Will took it all in, considering the possibilities.

He could climb the copper beech and look for cater-pillars under the dark bronze leaves while he dreamed of building a tree house. He could take all his baseball cards to the arbor and sort them out on the flagstones, by team, or by position, or best to worst. He could pretend he was on a lone mission to dynamite enemy headquarters—usu-ally the compost heap—and make it out just in time to crawl back to base, dramatically wounded, and feed on ripe raspberries until his strength returned. Or he could mash up a potion of crabgrass, pond water, dandelions, and milkweed until it was a rich, evil green, just right for playing Warlocks and Witches with Anne and Emily.

But Anne and Emily had not wanted to play anything with him lately. They were always whispering together, or huddled over a book that they wouldn't let him see.

"You're too little," Emily had said, snatching the book away the one time he'd managed to place a hand on its worn cover. "It doesn't have any pictures."

For weeks, one or the other had carried the book everywhere. And yet it obviously didn't make them happy. Quite the contrary, they got crosser and crosser. Once when they were in the hammock, he snuck up on them through the secret passage and overheard Anne complaining, "It still says not yet, but it's been two whole weeks and nothing's happened. I can't stand it!"

When he emerged from the shrubs to ask, "Can't stand what?" they angrily told him to go away and mind his own business.

At first it didn't matter much, because he spent most of his time at Aaron Bach's down the block, playing ball with him and Pete, Aaron's cousin from Milwaukee. But at the beginning of July the Bachs left in a camper for the Wisconsin northwoods, where they were meeting Pete's folks at their cabin. It seemed all his other friends were somewhere on vacation, too, or at day camp. Will hadn't even thought of asking to go to camp, because last summer had been so much fun.

Last summer, Anne and Emily had enlisted him as a squire in a running game of King Arthur and his knights, and when he got tired of waiting on Sir Lancelot and Sir Gawain, they let him have a turn at jousting. He rode the tire swing with an old broomstick lance under his arm, trying to knock over a target made from cardboard boxes, flower stakes, and duct tape. They'd played Robin Hood, too, and when he objected to always being the rich bad guy who got tied to a tree, Anne said he could be the sheriff and have a sword, and she had drawn a mustache on his upper lip with Magic Marker (actually, it turned out to be an indelible laundry pen, but Will was secretly pleased with the shadow that lingered for days after his mother's scrubbing).

But Will's favorite game had been Warlocks and Witches. He got to travel on dangerous quests to find the right ingredients for magic potions, like dragon's blood and goblin's slime (the blood came from squashing a gypsy moth caterpillar and the slime was a slug—both destructive garden pests and thus fair game). Often he was Zindar, a rebel warlock who challenged the power of the evil Lord Deathlock (Anne), entering into an uneasy alliance with the powerful Witch of Timberfell (also Anne) and the Azalea Elves (all played by Emily).

There was double-crossing and triple-crossing, stealthy invasions through the secret passage, and the chanting of magic spells over a luscious collection of potions prepared in any receptacle that fell to hand. (They had confined themselves mostly to old jars and tin cans, though, ever since their father, reaching for ice cubes for his evening scotch, stuck his fingers into a tray filled with cold green ooze. He was not mollified to learn that it had to be frozen for a spell that would bring storms of winter down on the Azalea Elves.)

The best thing about the game was that Will wasn't

just an extra. He knew plants and insects better than Anne and Emily. He could always use his knowledge in the changing plot, like the time he showed Emily where to find dozens of potato bugs under a rotten stump behind the garage, and they turned them into warriors who attacked Lord Deathlock by night.

He sighed, leaning his elbows on the warm sill, and heard the creak-bang of the back screen door. His mother had gone inside. Now she was moving around in the kitchen under his room, opening and closing cupboards. The rest of the house was quiet. Anne and Emily were probably still asleep, or whispering so softly over that dumb book that he couldn't hear them across the hall.

And then, looking down through the leafy branches of the beech, Will saw the book. It was lying in the hammock, completely vulnerable. Somehow, Anne and Emily must have forgotten it there last night when they were called in to bed.

It took only a moment for him to creep down the stairs and out the back door with his sneakers in his hand, dodging through the kitchen as his mother whirred the coffee grinder with her back turned. He scooped up the book from the hammock and kept right on going, padding barefoot past the azaleas to the middle of the secret passage. There was just room for him to sit down, leaning his back against the garage wall, and be completely hidden from view by the shrubbery.

He parted the book's pages at random, letting them fall open in his lap. "No pictures," Emily had said. What a lie! He'd opened to two pages full of pictures, and in color, too. Then he stared, too surprised to breathe.

The pictures were in little boxes, in sequence, like a comic. And there in the first one was a boy who looked just like him, Will Thornton, lying in a bed that looked exactly like his own. You could even see baseball cards among the sheets, and the encyclopedia open on the floor. The next box showed his mother gardening—at least she wore the same kind of hat and had the same unruly hair. And then came a picture of the boy standing at a window, and a glorious double panel that showed a garden, no, *the* garden, *his* garden; there was just no question about it. And almost hidden in the folds of the hammock in the bottom left corner of the picture, he could make out the book, drawn very small, but as unmistakable as it had been when he'd seen it in real life from the window.

On the facing page came pictures of the boy sneaking down the stairs, grabbing the book from the hammock, and opening it behind some bushes. Breathing too fast now, Will turned the page.

The next picture was a full-page portrait of a strange

little man peering out from a large hawthorn bush. His face was smooth and taut, like the skin of an apple, and his eyes were bright and curious as a bird's. Cocked at an angle on his head was a three-cornered hat made of copper beech leaves. He wore a furry, quilted vest of brown and gold, stitched, it seemed, out of a dozen caterpillar skins, and his greenish trousers had a snakeskin sheen. They were tucked into tall boots the color of birch bark, and belted with grass-green braid. One of his hands was hidden by the hawthorn leaves, but the other, sinewy and brown, clutched a knobby staff.

Will studied the illustration, assessing the expression on the little man's face and trying to estimate his size. He looked inquisitive and sly, like a trickster waiting to see his mischief at work. And judging from the size of the leaves on the hawthorn, he couldn't be bigger than, oh, the span of Will's hand.

Suddenly a twig snapped, and Will looked up from the book just in time to see the little man in the picture look him right in the eye, with the same mischievous expression on his face. In an instant he had turned and disappeared into the leaves, a cocoon-shaped knapsack bouncing on his back as he ran.

And without a moment's hesitation, Will dropped the book and dived into the bush after him.

"WELCOME TO JARDINIA"

 The thorny bush Will dived into was far bigger and darker than he'd expected. In fact, it was more like a jungle or a forest than a bush, he thought, peering up at the pale, green light that filtered through the thick canopy of leaves. Where the sunlight was strongest, a kind of exotic underbrush grew waist-high, the leaves big and jagged.

Then he heard a laugh like a bird's chirp, and

glimpsed the little man again, crouched behind a tangled patch of vines. He wasn't so little, actually. In fact, when he straightened up to run off again, he was almost Will's height, only more wiry.

Will pounded doggedly after him, feeling the earth cool and damp under his bare feet. He was gaining steadily, eyes fixed on the knapsack jiggling ahead, when suddenly a shaft of sunlight nearly blinded him. With a sweep of his staff, the little man had parted the thorny branches and brought bright daylight flooding in. Then, quick as a wink, he slipped through the gap he'd made and let the branches brush closed behind him.

Huge thorns tore at Will's short-sleeved summer pajama top as he tried to follow, and his hands and arms were scratched bloody. But he finally emerged into bright sunshine, dazed and staring.

He was in another world. He stood at the edge of a vast prairie, where the thick, shoulder-high grass rippled like water in the breeze. Prehistoric creatures hovered on the horizon. One looked a bit like the pterodactyl in his dinosaur book, another like a winged dragon. They hovered and swooped, swooped and hovered, and the green and purple dragon-thing spread glittery rainbow wings in the sun while Will watched in amazement. For an instant, he thought of *Anax junius*, the green darner depicted in his insect book. But he dismissed the idea. Green darners were large, for dragonflies, as much as three inches long, but this creature was as big as he was.

Suddenly, out of the corner of his eye, he saw something black, about the size of a dachshund, darting through the grass a few steps away. It paused and waved black antennae at him before hurrying off.

"Doesn't look like a prince," complained a gruff voice nearby.

"Doesn't look like much of a fighter, neither," said a small, squeaky voice.

"Looks like a kid, if you ask me, Mockerskin," a third said flatly.

Will turned this way and that, but he couldn't see anyone.

"Well, beggars can't be choosers, y' know," retorted a fourth voice, and the speaker chiruped a birdlike laugh. "Had to take what came along. Had to play it by the book, so to speak." And he laughed again.

Then Will saw them. They were sitting on a hawthorn branch above his head, four of them. One was the little man he'd chased—Mockerskin, they'd called him. The others sat next to him, smallest to biggest.

"Psst! He sees us, Spiderwort," Mockerskin said out of the corner of his mouth to the thin little fellow at his side, who wore a cobweb-gray suit with a hood.

"He's listening, Hackberry," squeaked Spiderwort,

shivering and clutching the arm of the stout, scarlet-clad fellow on his left. Hackberry's broad face flushed as red as his clothes.

"Just as I said, Bullthistle, nothing but a kid," he announced to the last and tallest man, who looked mournfully at Will from under a tuft of stiff white hair, and stroked his downy beard.

"What's going on here?" demanded Will. "Where am I anyway?"

There was some whispered consultation, and Will heard Bullthistle's gravelly voice say, "Yes, but no more than he needs to know." And then suddenly they all leaped down beside him, leaving the hawthorn branch shaking overhead.

"Welcome to Jardinia," said Bullthistle, who seemed to be the oldest. "We're Gnomblins," he added, bowing. "The g is silent, but we rarely are, I'm afraid. Sorry about the bad manners. It's just that we didn't know what the champion would look like, and you aren't quite what we expected. What's your name?"

"Will Thornton," he answered, automatically shaking Bullthistle's hand, which was calloused and rough to the touch. "What do you mean, champion?"

But before he even got the question out, Spiderwort started to prance about in excitement, piping, "Will

Thornton—it fits, it fits!" And Hackberry was pumping his hand, saying, "So sorry I doubted you, sir."

Will was increasingly annoyed. There was nothing he hated more than not understanding the conversation, unless it was being told "You're too little" or "Never mind, Will, it's too complicated" when he asked for an explanation. Also, he was beginning to feel hungry.

"Let's explain the whole thing over breakfast," Bullthistle said quickly, as though sensing Will's feelings. "Hackberry and Mockerskin, please set out the picnic while I begin the story. Spiderwort, can you manage the umbrella?"

The three others scurried off into the shadow of the bush again, and reappeared moments later. Hackberry had his arms full of pouches and sacks, and Mockerskin was dragging a thick square of soft, mossy green—the picnic blanket. Spiderwort brought up the rear, almost completely hidden by an enormous buff-colored umbrella that he was half pushing, half carrying before him. It looked remarkably like a toadstool, except ten times too big.

"Perhaps I should start with the rune," said Bullthistle, who had invited Will to sit down on a fallen log, and seated himself heavily beside him. "Passed down from father to daughter and mother to son, you might say, as far

back as it goes, to be used in Jardinia's greatest hour of
need.

>"*Pluck the thorn and not the rose*
>*For when there's a will, there's a way*
>*Catch a prince to face your foes*
>*For when there's a will there's a way*
>*The champion must fight where the water flows*
>*For when there's a will, there's a way*
>*Climb high and see as do the crows*
>*For when there's a will, there's a way.*"

When he'd finished intoning the rhyme, Bullthistle
paused significantly, eyeing Will.

Spiderwort, who had abandoned the umbrella, waved
his pale, tapered hands excitedly. "Don't you see?" he
asked. " 'When there's a *Will*'! That's you. 'Pluck the
thorn.' That's you again. "Thorn-ton. Can't be an accident. And Mockerskin caught you, all right."

"Be quiet!" rumbled Bullthistle. He turned to Will
and his expression became even graver. "Will Thornton,"
he said, "you were sent to save Jardinia in her time of
greatest danger. Only you can break the terrible spell
that has been cast over our land by the evil enchanter
Forficula."

He gestured out toward the prairie, which stretched as far as the eye could see.

"Ten days ago, this was a neat little lawn, and those fearsome creatures flying overhead were merely insects. Then Forficula cast a growing curse on Jardinia, and everything began to expand, swelling grotesquely day by day, or, rather, night by night; everything, from ants and earthworms to wolf spiders—except us Gnomblins, the natural guardians of Jardinia. By now, it is all ten times too big, and our very existence is threatened."

Will squinted at the horizon. So it *had* been a green darner, he thought, with a shiver of excitement. It was as though the magnified photographs in his insect book had come to life, bigger and more exquisitely detailed than the real things ever were. He'd love to see a ten-times-too-big lacewing, or a Silver-spotted Skipper, that darting, elusive insect that looked so charming in the book, with its round black eye and the silvery splash on its soft brown wings. But a wolf spider—*ugh*. Not to mention wasps, hornets, and mosquitoes. Why, a bite from a mosquito ten times too big could probably leave you weak from loss of blood, and turn your whole body into an itchy welt!

"There are some advantages, of course," said Mocker-skin, carefully opening his knapsack and taking out something wrapped in leaves. It turned out to be an enormous ripe raspberry, only slightly bruised from bouncing in the backpack, and it gave off a mouth-watering perfume. "But I had to fight off a dozen giant ants to harvest this beauty. Want a slice?"

He and Hackberry had set the umbrella-toadstool into a circular hole cut into the center of the mossy square, and had already unpacked most of the pouches and sacks. Besides the raspberry, luminescent with sweet juice, there was an acorn bowl holding several hulled sunflower seeds the size of cookies, honeysuckle trumpets overflowing with sweet water, a salad of mint leaves, and assorted roots, which Hackberry crunched happily like carrots.

"Crudités," he told Will. "Have one. Full of vitamins. Make you grow."

Will declined the root politely, but gladly accepted a glistening section of raspberry on a plate-sized leaf. It was delicious, and so juicy you had to slurp as you ate, or the juice trickled, red and sticky, down your front. No one seemed to mind.

"Forficula," Will said consideringly when he'd finished his piece of raspberry, spitting out the pips like grape seeds as he saw the others do. "Sounds kind of familiar to me, but I can't think why."

Mockerskin drained his honeysuckle and brushed the crumbs from his vest.

"A creature of the night, who commands the armies of Death Mountain," he said. "And he can't take a joke."

"You and your jokes," squealed Spiderwort. "If it hadn't been for your stupid joke with the stinkbugs, we wouldn't be in this mess."

Mockerskin looked abashed for an instant, but then he crinkled up his eyes in suppressed glee.

"I just wish I could have seen his face when he opened the box," he said. "Expecting imported fireflies to twinkle for his nasty guests and instead setting loose a legion of stinkbugs to fumigate them. I'm glad I spoiled Forficula's coronation."

"Is he a king, then?" asked Will.

"Worse," put in Hackberry. "Says he's an emperor. Emperor of Jardinia. Never was an emperor in Jardinia. Never will be if we Gnomblins have anything to do with it. Certainly not an emperor like him!" Hackberry shuddered.

"What's he like?" Will persisted.

The four Gnomblins eyed one another uneasily.

"Tell him, Bullthistle," squeaked Spiderwort.

Bullthistle furrowed his bristly eyebrows and studied Will carefully.

"You have a right to the truth," he said at last in his deep voice. "But Forficula is not easy to describe.

"Think of dampness and decay. Think of mold, and

the phosphorescence of slime. Think of cruel pincers and many legs scuttling in the dark. That's what Forficula's like. He grows bigger night by night, with great slimy, hornlike tentacles protruding from his head and a sheath of dark-brown body armor beneath his huge cloak. He slithers and scuttles when he moves, and he leaves behind a mucuslike smear that withers and rots all it touches. The cloak itself is leprous with mold, but though it crumbles to the touch, it seems to renew itself by spreading mold in turn to anything it touches.

"Mockerskin said he would have liked to see Forficula's face, but it was only a manner of speaking. Forficula has no face as you and I know the word. He waves those slime-shiny pincers of his to and fro like antennae, because he is eyeless. Yet his senses are so keen, he can spot a falling primrose petal in the night before it touches earth. With one sweep of his cloak, it is his, another tidbit to add to Death Mountain.

"And what a mountain! Towering and sprawling and spreading the smell of death, yet alive with Forficula's nocturnal armies, who are as evil a pack of scavenging bloodsuckers as you'd want to meet on a moonless night. Scorpion flies, robber flies, earwigs, pinacate beetles— hundreds of them, now grossly swollen to many times their natural size, so that any two of them could overcome even an armed Gnomblin. And that, Will Thornton, is why we need you."

Bullthistle's voice rumbled to a stop. The other Gnomblins turned and looked at Will expectantly. He felt hot and cold at the same time. It was the way he felt when his first-grade teacher, Mrs. Dimwittie, called on him to read, and, in the classroom's terrible waiting silence, all the black letters swam at him, impenetrable and urgent.

"What on earth am I supposed to do?" he asked, hoping his voice didn't sound too wobbly.

"Face 'em down, like the rune says," said Hackberry.

"You're the champion," piped up Spiderwort. "You could always use your human magic."

"Don't be such a snerd, you spidersquirt," Mockerskin told Spiderwort. "He isn't magic himself, just the instrument of magic."

"Quiet!" roared Bullthistle, so loudly that Will jumped. Then he put a reassuring hand on Will's shoulder. "Do you like riddles?" he asked gently. "I thought so. Now listen carefully.

"Three things are needed to break the spell, one from earth, one from water, and one from air. This we learned from the sphinx moths, who know more than they tell, but tell more than they should. And the following riddle, they say, is true about each thing:

"Too small to see, in death I live;
In life I die, and life I give.

"The first can only be found in Forficula's realm of Death Mountain. The second is at the center of the Lake of Stone Shores. And the third is found in the air of Break Neck Cliff. But don't worry about the other two now. For each quest we have special weapons and help to give you. If you are brave and quick-witted—and we know you are—you will prevail, just as the rune promises, and Jardinia will be saved."

Will was no coward. His curiosity had always been stronger than his fear, even when he was a baby, crawling or toddling after the unfamiliar with such speed that his mother lost him half a dozen times before his third birthday. But this Death Mountain business was all a little too much.

"You know, I really should be getting home," he said hastily. "I mean, I'd love to help you guys, really I would, but I don't know that particular riddle, and my moth . . . uh, people will be looking for me by this time. I mean, thanks for the meal and all, but I've really gotta go."

The Gnomblins said nothing. Nobody tried to stop him when he stepped into the bush, looking for a path, any path, through the tangle of branches.

The thorns seemed to grow thicker and sharper before his eyes, and the harder he tried to push through, the tighter the branches were entwined, as though they were actually barring his way. He fell back and turned to face the four Gnomblins. From their expressions, Will could tell that they had known all along he couldn't leave. Suddenly he remembered the way little Spiderwort had crowed, "And Mockerskin caught you, all right!"

"There's only one way home for you now, lad," Bullthistle said softly. "And it runs through Death Mountain."

THE SORCERER
OF DEATH MOUNTAIN

Emily remembered the book the moment she woke up. How could she have left it in the hammock? What if it had rained in the night? She imagined it splotched and soggy, the little magic it had left washed away, or puddling uselessly in the grass.

Throwing back the sheet, she tore out of bed, ran from the room she shared with Anne, which faced the street, and to the window on the staircase landing. She was just in time to see Will disappear into the secret passage. But Will didn't interest her. She craned her neck to see the hammock, and with a sinking heart realized it was empty.

It took Emily only a few moments to shake Anne awake and ask if she had brought in the book. When Anne said no, it took only an instant more for Emily to remember the sight of Will disappearing into the secret passage. Hadn't he been clutching something in his hand?

But by the time they had run downstairs and out into the garden, and thrashed through the secret passage like a couple of wild boars, Will was gone.

It was Anne who saw the book, open and sticking out from under a shrub.

"Aha!" she cried triumphantly, thinking Will had thrown it there and run away when he heard them coming. And then, with a stab of fear, she saw the pictures.

"He's gone, Em," she said. "Look, that's him following that elf or whatever he is, and the rest of the pages don't turn. He's disappeared into his own adventure."

Emily felt frightened and angry at the same time.

"He's too little to go off on his own like that," she said indignantly. "And the book is ours, not his. He doesn't even have a clue how to handle the magic."

For the moment she had forgotten that she and Anne were not exactly masters at handling the magic either.

Anne slumped against the garage, staring at the last picture.

"I don't like it, Emily. It makes me think of stories about elves and goblins stealing children. I mean, look at these pictures. He was lured away. And we have the book here—he didn't take it with him. How is he going to get back?"

A lump filled Emily's throat. She was remembering how mean she'd been to Will in the last weeks. Maybe they had been meant to share the book with him all along, and that's why it hadn't worked for her and Anne a second time. Maybe the magic had refused to cooperate with them because Will was supposed to have a turn. Or was the reason more sinister?

She had a sudden image of Will as a baby, beating his arms in the air with excitement over a smile or word from her, his whole face alight with joy. She remembered his downy hair, like fuzz on a new chick, and the sad little baby bye-bye wave he would make when she left for nursery school. He would call plaintively after her, "Blee, blee," because that was as close as he could come to saying "Emily."

"Will!" she called, starting to cry. "Will, where are you? Come back!"

There was no reply, only the humming stillness of the garden in the morning sun.

＊

"One suit of carabid armor," Hackberry was saying, pulling something black and shiny from a sack. It seemed to be a kind of breastplate fashioned from the shell of some enormous beetle. "One leather belt. One spider's net—careful, it's sticky, you know. Three poison fume pellets in a pouch; see, there's also a side pocket you can use to carry away what you need to break the spell, once you've figured out what that is."

"*Too small to see, in death I live,*" shrilled Spiderwort. "But if it's too small to see, how can he see to put it in the pouch?"

Will thought that was a very sensible question, but Bullthistle hushed the smaller Gnomblin, as usual, and Hackberry continued his inventory of Will's tools and weapons.

"One slingshot, with missiles." The missiles were spiked, like horse chestnuts. "Two flares; they light on impact. Very precious, they are. Use only when absolutely necessary. You can't imagine how hard it is getting the firefly juice to make 'em. Now, let's see what's left in here . . . Yes, one pouch of polished pebbles. Come in handy, they do. One night mask; helps you to see in the dark. Ah, here we are, finally: one silver sword, sharpened. There's the scabbard for it, too."

Will reached for the sword eagerly. He'd never seen anything more beautiful. Its blade and silver handle flashed in the sun the way pretend swords of plastic never do. The scabbard was made of leather, but stamped with an intricate design of green and silver, like stylized leaves entwining crescent moons. The hilt curved toward his hand, and it, too, was embossed with the leaf-and-moon design.

Will sheathed the sword, then drew it out again swiftly, enjoying its perfect balance and the way the air sighed when he sliced through it. He almost forgot that he had tried to go home, the sword made him feel so brave.

The rest of the day was spent in practice and preparation. Will soon got the hang of the slingshot after Hackberry showed him how to put a spin on the spiky ammunition; it was a little like a knuckleball pitch.

But the spider's net was trickier. Time and again Spiderwort demonstrated its use. He launched the filmy mass so that it unreeled in one smooth motion, ballooned out as it fell, and—at another flick of the wrist—drew tight again, capturing the enemy. When Will tried it he got tangled up in it himself, and found the gossamer threads of the net surprisingly strong and unpleasantly sticky. Eventually he learned to use it without such mishaps, but it still tended to flop to the ground half-open, instead of soaring up and stretching wide enough to capture one of Forficula's scuttling squadrons.

"Not to worry, not to worry," Spiderwort insisted, after scampering back from the far edge of Will's last and best try. "You have the arm and the eye right, and that extra snap of the wrist"—here he flopped his thin hands back and forth, making a face so scared and silly that Will had to laugh—"well, next to practice, there's nothing like a bit of danger for the knack."

After a refreshing lunch break of cold blackberry soup, Mockerskin instructed him in the use of the fume pellets, which were a little like grenades or smoke bombs. They emitted a gas that temporarily paralyzed those who breathed it. The trick was to be sure which way the wind was blowing, pull the pin with your teeth, and heave the pellet far enough downwind so you wouldn't be overcome yourself. Will couldn't practice with the real thing, of course, but he used stones. By the time the evening breeze began to blow, he was quite adept at reading the grass and leaves for wind direction, positioning himself, and pitching a pretend pellet just so.

"How about the sword?" he asked when the late afternoon shadows were growing long. "Shouldn't I practice with the sword?"

"No practice needed," said Bullthistle. "That sword's your very own and true, and in the moonlight it will do what you will, Will."

Mockerskin erupted in laughter at the weak pun, and for several minutes thereafter Spiderwort could be heard trying it out under his breath:

"What you will, Will. What you, Will, will," and even, "Will you will it, Will?" until Will told him to knock it off, or he would have a few things to say about the name Spiderwort.

Not a moment too soon, Bullthistle announced that it was time for tiffin. In Jardinia, that turned out to mean sharing an early evening snack of chopped apples, nuts, and honey from a shallow stone bowl still warm from the sun's last rays. The ceremonial meal served as a chance to recall the happenings of an important day, and to lay to rest any quarrels.

As they sat in a circle and took turns scooping, Bullthistle explained that the four had been entrusted with finding Will and outfitting him for battle because of their special talents. Spiderwort was quick and nimble with the spider's net. Plainspoken, stalwart Hackberry excelled at the slingshot, and Mockerskin, a master of trickery and disguise, knew all about poisons, especially gases. Bullthistle himself was considered tough but wise, and steeped in the old ways of rune and legend.

Generally Gnomblins are homebodies, he said, never straying far from the raspberry groves where most of them live. But when the Gnomblins understood the impact of Forficula's curse, the four were chosen to venture out in search of the champion foretold by the ancient rune.

"We can accompany you as far as the gray wasteland, and we'll wait there for your return," he told Will. "But beyond that, you must go alone. After the wasteland comes a grassy place, and then a gully full of underbrush. On the other side of the gully is Death Mountain. Your quest can only be completed in the night, so we should all try to get some sleep now. We'll start out after dark."

To his surprise, Will found it quite easy to fall asleep on the soft picnic moss. In place of his earlier fear he felt a kind of resolute calm. He could feel events unfolding in the rhythm of his favorite fairy tales, the ones in which the youngest of three children succeeds against all the odds after the others have failed to slay the dragon or scale the glass mountain.

It was pitch-black when he was awakened, but Mockerskin soon slipped the night mask over Will's face. The mask was stiff and furry, with pointed edges like a bat's ears. Will found he could see quite well through its eye slits, though it gave everything a heightened, surreal quality, like a scene played under strobe lights.

The carabid armor was surprisingly light. Spiderwort fastened breastplate and backplate together with his deft little fingers, while Hackberry helped Will buckle on the wide belt from which the various pouches and pellets dangled. The spider's net, tightly reeled and tied to a flexible wooden rod, was slung over his shoulder. Last came the sword, and once again Will felt his heart lift when he touched its hilt.

They started out single file, Bullthistle in the lead and Will close behind, keeping to the edge of what he now thought of as jungle, and skirting the tall prairie grass on the other side. Will had the impression they were moving downhill, first gradually, then more steeply. At last they reached a valley where the prairie grass grew more sparsely.

"We're close to the gray wasteland now," Bullthistle said in a hoarse whisper. "Watch your step."

"What's that?" gasped Will as something lumbered away in the grass. The thing was more than a foot long, black and bomb-shaped, carried by half a dozen shiny black legs.

"Probably a straggler from Forficula's army," Bullthistle replied. "Pinacate beetle, from the looks of him—part of the Poison Gas Brigade. Horrible, the stench they can make together, and harmful to a Gnomblin's lungs, but not a human's, we think."

Behind the night mask, Will's eyes widened. "Wait a minute," he said.

He suddenly thought of his father's reading voice, slow and deep, coming over his left shoulder as he sat leaning against his father's broad chest, a book open before them.

"If you continue to bother it, the beetle will release a blackish, foul-smelling fluid," his father was reading. "Pinacate beetles are also called olive beetles, because they look something like black olives, and, for obvious reasons, another name is 'stink beetles.' "

Will never failed to laugh at the picture of the "stinky black olive." But magnified ten times over, he thought now, it looked less like a smelly appetizer than a deadly weapon.

As they continued weaving their way through the grass, he tried to summon up whatever else he knew about these insects. They emerge at dusk, he remembered, live up to three years in open, grassy areas and dry woodlands, and eat . . . What *did* they eat?

Bullthistle stopped short and put out a restraining arm.

"We're here," he said, and pointed.

Two feet ahead, the grass abruptly ended, along with all other signs of life. Even the earth, damp and uneven under their muffled tread, stopped short at the edge of a vast desert of gray stone. Just then the moon broke through the clouds. Refracted through the night mask, its light so dazzled Will that he was momentarily blinded.

"Quick, take it off," Bullthistle told him. "But keep it with you, for if the moon dims again you'll need it more than ever. We shall wait for you here, by the square oak."

Only then did Will notice a great trunk at the rim of the wasteland. But it was unlike any oak he'd ever seen, a massive, square-sided thing that rose straight up and disappeared into darkness.

"Make haste while the moon shines," Bullthistle urged, his white tuft of hair almost silver in the moonlight. "Straight north is the shortest way. Here," he added, and fumbling in a pocket, he withdrew a saucer-sized compass. "Take this to guide you, for it is said the stars do not shine over the wasteland, and the constellations will be of no help."

When Will answered, his voice sounded thin and lost echoing out over the stony vastness.

"How will I know what to bring back?" he asked, as he had many times already that day.

"Face your foes, Will, and the rest will follow," replied

Bullthistle again. "You'll know what to do when the time comes."

The others clustered around him for a moment. Hackberry put a broad palm on his back; Mockerskin's face twitched between a grin and a grimace; and Spiderwort hopped from one leg to the other, quavering, "Oh, good luck, Will, good luck!"

※

It was hard underfoot, and the chill penetrated the thick boots Hackberry had given him. For a while Will still heard the Gnomblins' voices through his own hollow footsteps, calling out goodbyes and good wishes. Then the voices grew too faint to understand. And finally, when he paused, he could hear nothing at all but the terrible, lonely silence of stone.

He felt more alone than he had in his life. He thought fleetingly of his parents, then of Anne and Emily. He imagined them all very small, distant figures in a boat at sea, and himself stranded on an enormous beach at low tide, watching the boat bob away toward the far horizon.

He began to run. His boots were so loud on the stone surface that he couldn't hear anything else. But suddenly he realized the dull moonlit shine of the stone floor was dimming. He glanced up as he ran, thinking a cloud had covered the moon.

The first instant, it was like looking into a dark chasm without edges, into nothingness. Then he became aware that the darkness itself was mottled and moving. It was gathering thickness like an evil cloud above him. He stopped, instinctively cringing under his upraised arm. He heard the beat, beat, beat of a hundred wings closing in.

Before he could scream, they swooped down on him: dozens of giant moths with huge, smothering wings. He cried out, waving his arms wildly, and they retreated a little. But they regrouped and descended once more, surrounding him in a relentless, fluttering mass.

Light, he thought. *I need light.* He tore at one of two egg-shaped flares hanging from his belt. Hackberry had warned him to save them for emergencies, but surely this counted as one.

He hurled the flare to one side. It exploded, sending up a pillar of greenish light that illuminated the wasteland like a lightning bolt. For a split second, Will longed for the darkness again. Now he could see the thick, ugly bodies of the moths between their brown wings. The stone desert looked even harsher and more unyielding in the light.

Then the moths veered, drawn as though by a powerful magnet to the flare. Before the phosphorescent glow could fade, Will aimed a poison fume pellet at the spot,

hoping that he was out of range and that no sudden wind would send the gas back to him. Clenching the pin in his teeth, he watched the pellet shatter.

It sent smoke billowing high among the beating wings. In an instant the moths faltered and began falling to the ground, a thudding rain of fat brown bodies and rigid wings paralyzed into helplessness.

Will sprinted away from the downed moths with new confidence, following the arrow of his compass. He ran for a long time, panting. The pouches bumped against his thighs and the sword in its scabbard danced at his side. Finally he stopped to listen again and to scan the horizon. Twice he ran like that until he was winded. Twice he listened only to his own breathing and saw nothing except gray wasteland in all directions. But the third time he heard the scrabble, scrabble, scrabble of hundreds of sharp claws against stone. The sound sent a chill of fear right through him.

In the far distance, he thought he could make out the end of the wasteland in the scraggly outline of some weed or bush. But hard by, on his left flank and coming closer, was a turmoil of dark, crawling creatures. They were glossy black and purple, with narrow heads, long antennae, and powerful, protruding jaws. If each had been small enough to fit on Will's palm he wouldn't have hesitated to identify them as ground beetles, family *Carabidae*. But they were the size of violin cases—the kind where gangsters hide machine guns.

"The best way to see these common beetles is to go out at night with a flashlight," his insect book had advised. "They are very active as they search for insect prey."

For the first time, Will envisioned himself as an insect grub, a tempting morsel to be ripped at by saw-toothed mandibles.

"Okay, guys," he said out loud to steady his nerves, unslinging the spider's net. "Come and get it."

This time he could feel he'd done his job right, flicking the net over and out in a singing arc, the way his uncle Paul had once taught him to cast for trout. The net opened wide and fell perfectly, enveloping the scrambling battalion of predators in tough, sticky filaments. Will pulled in tight, forcing the giant beetles together in a struggling heap, and knotted the reel end the way Spiderwort had shown him.

Only two of the creatures escaped the net's folds. Will faced them down, sword in hand, and they scurried away.

Turning northward once more, Will saw the clear edge of the wasteland in the moonlight. He was so glad to find earth and grass underfoot again that he forgot for a moment that it meant he was drawing close to Death

Mountain and the evil sorcerer Forficula. But when he reached the gully of which Bullthistle had spoken, he took cover in the underbrush.

He needed cunning and cleverness now, not just courage. Even if he could single-handedly defeat Forficula and the rest of his armies, what good would it do if he couldn't figure out what to seize and carry back?

Too small to see, in death I live; / In life I die, and life I give. The words went round and round in his head, meaningless, maddening, like the high-pitched drone of a mosquito. And in a resounding bass counterpoint, he imagined he heard Bullthistle's commanding voice repeating, over and over, "Face your foes, Will. Face your foes."

He inched through the underbrush and crawled up the steep side of the gully. There it was, the smell Bullthistle had described, but stronger and more penetrating than Will could have imagined. Dampness and decay, the Gnomblin had said. But that wasn't all. To his surprise, Will was reminded of the deep, rich smell of earth in the rain. He suddenly thought of his mother digging up a clump of irises to divide and replant them after a summer thunderstorm, her hands heavy with black dirt.

Slowly, he edged forward, taking care to stay hidden. At last, parting the curtain of underbrush at the top of the gully, he saw it: Death Mountain.

It slouched against the star-filled sky like a hump-backed monster, sprawling out to the edges of Will's field of vision as though to blot out the landscape of living things. But instead of deathly silence, Will heard the rustling and scuttling and—could it be?—the *chewing* of an enormous army.

The moon, which he had been unable to see over the wasteland, now sailed into view at the rim of the mountain, shining round as a silver dollar. But for the first time, Will saw the familiar shadows on the moon's surface as decay—a moldy, destructive contagion spread by the hump-backed mountain of death below.

Gripping his gleaming sword hilt for reassurance, he scanned the moonlit terrain for clues to the Gnomblin riddle. There was something at the back of his mind, something to do with irises, if he could only remember . . .

Then he was jumped from behind. He struggled to draw his sword as a cold, serpentlike thing wound itself around him. Wrenching himself free, he brought the sword out of its scabbard and slashed down on his attacker, slicing it in two. To his horror, the two bloodied pieces continued to slither toward him. He pierced them repeatedly, and finally they lay still.

With a rush of relief and embarrassment, he realized that he had been battling an earthworm. An outsized earthworm, to be sure, but still a worm, and probably no more dangerous than the night crawlers he used to bait his fishing hook. But the duel had eliminated any hope of remaining hidden, he figured. Forficula probably had sentries guarding the outskirts of his domain, and they had no doubt seen him by now.

Sure enough, there was a flurry at the edge of the mountain. Then the mountain itself seemed to tremble. It heaved and broke open, and from the blackness within issued a torrent of pinacate beetles. The Poison Gas Brigade!

A gas mask was what he needed, but that hadn't been part of Hackberry's arsenal. How much could he do with his sword against so many, especially if the Gnomblins were wrong about human lungs tolerating pinacate fumes?

He wet a finger and held it to the air, as Mockerskin had taught him. Just as he feared, the breeze was blowing the wrong way. The pinacate gases would be wafted straight at him, and so would the poison fumes of his remaining pellets if he threw them now. In desperation, he tore up a fistful of grass and pressed it to his face, breathing in the sweet smell as though it could shield him. He thought of retreating to the bottom of the gully, but the recollection of Bullthistle's words stopped him. *Face your foes, Will. The rest will follow.*

With a fierce cry, Will charged at the beetle swarm, his sword held high. They froze, spreading their legs and pointing their bomb-shaped abdomens skyward. But before they could loose their foul fluid, a terrible voice rang from the depths of the mountain.

"Halt," it rasped, drawing out the word so it scraped against the air like metal on stone. "Bring him here unharmed."

Where the mountain had broken open, a dark shadow emerged. It seemed to unfold, rising taller and taller, until it towered over the beetle army. More than twice as high as Will and much more massive, entirely swathed in a black cloak, Forficula himself was sliding from Death Mountain.

At the sorcerer's command, the beetles surged again, undeterred by Will's flashing sword. Will managed to flip the first ones that reached him, driving the sword into their soft underbellies. But there were too many of them. Climbing one on the other, they pressed closer, surrounding Will, pinning his sword arm against his side. They pushed him toward Forficula and the cleft that yawned in Death Mountain.

Will was almost as angry as he was frightened. He

hated bullies, and nearly seven years as the youngest in the family had made him sensitive to being shoved around.

"Who do you think you are?" he demanded of the black-draped figure when he was deposited in front of him. Without thinking, Will took the few blades of grass still clutched in his left fist and threw them at the sorcerer.

Like a waiting predator, the black cloak pounced, swirling out to envelop the leaves of grass before they fell. Will heard a sound like moist lips smacking, and a few blackened strands fell to the ground near his feet.

"An offering for the Emperor. How . . . sweet," the voice said.

The sound made Will think of a corpse dragged over rough ground. Instinctively, he tried to step back. A hard, smooth wall of beetle shells was right behind him.

A growling chortle came from inside the cloak. "Can this be the much-vaunted Gnomblin champion? Or is it a clever ploy, the champion disguised as a small human child? A *very* small human child, indeed."

The flash of Will's silver sword gave answer. Will was never sure whether the gleaming blade hadn't acted on its own, quicker than his arm, quicker than thought itself. It slashed into the huge cloak, and with its sharp bite of silver, the black thickness fell away, crumbling into moldy tatters that made the ground steam and darken where they dropped.

In an instant, Forficula stood revealed as Bullthistle had described him: a dark armored body that quivered now with rage; an eyeless head, and, protruding from it, slimy, wickedly curved pincers that groped for living flesh.

It was a terrifying image, but it was not unfamiliar.

"*Forficula auricularia*," Will breathed, remembering a picture in his insect book that was worth a shudder every time he saw it. The evil sorcerer, bane of Jardinia, was a gigantic, magically enhanced version of a European ear-wig.

"Its pincers are not just ornaments," the book had cautioned. "They can deliver a painful pinch if you try to handle one of these nocturnal visitors." And that had been written about earwigs half an inch long, not seven feet tall! A pinch from *these* cruel tentacles could crush the life out of him or slice him in two, Will was sure.

But in the moment of recognition came a new surge of confidence, and the vague but sharpening outline of an idea about the riddle's meaning. This was not the time to give up.

Will tore at the sack of pebbles hanging from his belt and sent the smooth, round stones rolling under the claws of the pinacate beetles at his back. Just as he'd hoped, they scuttled and skidded helplessly, giving him the chance he needed. Dodging the phosphorescent pincers that twisted down at him, Will used the flat of his sword to scoop up a blackened strand of grass and slide it into the side pocket of the pellet pouch. He was suddenly sure that in this bit of green blighted by Forficula was something he needed to break Jardinia's curse.

Then he rolled sideways, sword high, and heard Forficula hiss with anger to see his own Poison Gas Brigade totter, overpowered by a very small human boy with a bag of marbles.

"Air squadrons, attack!" the sorcerer rasped.

Scrambling toward the gully, Will heard the roar of wings fill the air. He looked back to see a cloud of giant robber flies rise from one side of the mountain. They were fierce, spiny-legged predators with beaklike mouthparts that they used to pierce their prey. From the other side came the blowflies, metallic green, with huge red eyes, the more horrible to Will because he knew they had grown from eggs hatched in dead flesh or garbage.

But the trick with the marbles had given him a head start, and as he turned to face the squadrons, he felt the wind shift just in time from his face to the sweat-soaked hair at the back of his neck. Moving his sword to his left hand, he pitched his two remaining poison pellets one after the other, with no time to correct his aim.

His eye hadn't failed him.

"Three strikes, you're out!" he yelled at Forficula, as the clouds of paralyzing smoke billowed up and converged over both squadrons, and giant insects rained down around the sorcerer.

But two robber flies from the far edge of the formation had escaped the poison fumes and continued to bear down on Will. Sheathing his sword, he grabbed the slingshot and sent a spiked missile spinning into the first one.

Zap! A direct hit. The robber fly staggered in its flight, turned, and spiraled helplessly to earth like a downed spitfire.

The second one was still coming, faster and faster. It was so close that Will could see its bulging, glossy black eyes and the razor-sharp bristles on its face and legs. There was no time to reload. Grasping a missile firmly between the spikes, Will hurled it with all his might and rocked back on his heels.

He had delivered the split-fingered fastball of his dreams: it hit the robber fly smack between the eyes. Then Will ran, and dived into the gully headfirst as though sliding home.

He scrambled out the other side on all fours. When he reached the wasteland, its stony emptiness was practically welcome after the fetid, swarming precincts of Death Mountain. You could almost say there was too much life for comfort inside Death Mountain, he thought. His boots rang rhythmically against the stone floor, and the pouch with its tiny cargo of decayed grass beat on his thigh, keeping time with the riddle that he now thought he understood.

Too small to see.

"It's the bacteria that does it," his mother had said, her hands full of black garden loam for the new iris bed she was planting. She was trying to explain how a haphazard pile of grass cuttings, dried leaves, and kitchen garbage—the compost heap—had yielded a wheelbarrow full of rich earth for her flowers. "Bacteria are tiny, tiny creatures," she went on, as he examined the dirt in the wheelbarrow skeptically. "They're too small to see, but quite powerful, really. They live off dead leaves, dead plants, orange rinds—any vegetable or fruit that was once alive."

In death I live.

Will had thrust both hands into the wheelbarrow, running the moist black leaf mold between his fingers. It smelled quite clean, like rain in the spring. Yet it was digested garbage, his mother was saying, transformed by the invisible bacteria into just the stuff the irises needed to flourish.

"But don't the bacterias eat up the flowers, too?" he'd asked, thinking of plant-devouring pests from aphids to Japanese beetles.

"No, darling, they don't eat living things," she'd reassured him. "But the bacteria can't live without dead plant waste to feed on, and the plants can't live without the nutritious waste the bacteria leave—you see, it's like a circle."

In life I die, and life I give.

Running through the moonlit night, Will was certain that some of those tiny creatures lay inside the pouch that thumped at his side, hidden within the black specks of decayed grass. Somehow, Forficula had harnessed—and distorted—the power of the magic circle that turned decay into growth.

But what Will carried in his pouch was only one of three ingredients needed to reverse the spell, he remembered—the one from earth. There was something from water, to be found in the Lake of Stone Shores, Bullthistle had said. And there was something from air, above the horribly named Break Neck Cliff.

Will was still straining to figure out the rest of the secret when the sky began to pale, and four familiar figures appeared as welcome shadows on the horizon.

"I've got it!" Will called out to them. "I've got it!"

And he laughed out loud to see the sky appear under Spiderwort's scrawny silhouette, as the smallest Gnomblin jumped up and down for joy.

FINDING WILL

𝒜nne and Emily crouched in the secret passage in front
of the open book for nearly half an hour, arguing about what
to do. Emily was in favor of shutting the book to try to bring
Will back. Anne was afraid that closing the covers on the
unopened pages might have the opposite effect.

"It could be like closing the only door out," she said.
"We could be sealing him in forever!"

When their mother called with an offer of breakfast, the issue was still undecided. For the time being, they agreed to put the book back under the hawthorn bush exactly as they had found it.

They were acutely conscious of the empty place at the breakfast table when they sat down to cereal and peaches, but to their astonishment their mother didn't ask about Will. Their father was deep in one of the three newspapers he read with his coffee, muttering now and then about the Middle East. He didn't even look up when Anne finally decided to risk the question: "Where's Will?"

"Oh, he's around somewhere," their mother said vaguely, screwing the top back on the raspberry jam. "Now, don't forget to clear the table and put the perishables in the fridge. I'll be in the study if you absolutely need me, but try to be independent this morning, because I'm writing a column about garden pests, and you know the subject makes me cross."

Their father lowered his newspaper long enough to kiss her before she left the room, then looked at his watch and yelped.

"I have to get going, kids," he said, popping the last piece of English muffin into his mouth. "The newsroom awaits. See you tonight. Be good."

It was a ritual that he kissed each of them goodbye

on both cheeks before he left for the office, oldest to youngest. Surely he would ask for Will now. But he didn't, and when Emily blurted out, "Will's gone, we can't find him," he gave a vague wave of his hand.

"Oh, Will was just here," he said placidly. "He's around somewhere."

Anne and Emily were used to their parents' absent-mindedness. Their mother, baking brownies for a school picnic, had once forgotten to put in the flour because she had her mind on seed catalogs. "I'm so sorry, darling," she'd told Emily, whose class picnic it was, "but they're delicious anyway. You could call them chocolate soufflé bars, don't you think?" And their father had once marinated a steak in liquid shoe polish instead of Worcestershire sauce because he was trying to make supper while talking on the telephone to the paper's correspondent in Manila.

But this was different.

"It's the magic," Anne told Emily after lunch, when their mother emerged to make them tuna sandwiches and again didn't ask after Will. "Grownups just don't notice he's gone."

"It's creepy," said Emily. "What if he never comes back? How can they go on not noticing?"

She tried to imagine Will's teacher, Mrs. Dimwittie, not noticing his absence in September. She was a large, beady-eyed woman who loudly enunciated every vowel and consonant as though speaking to hard-of-hearing Uzbekis, and she didn't miss much. But of course Will would have a new teacher in the fall. Perhaps he would simply be erased from the class list by the second week of school and fade from memory, like children who moved away over the summer. Perhaps eventually their own parents would forget him completely, leaving only Anne and Emily to mourn the little brother they'd once had.

By nightfall, these morbid thoughts were too much to bear. Repeated efforts to follow Will through the book had failed, and the pages still didn't turn beyond the illustration of his disappearance.

"Let's close the book," Anne said finally. "I can't stand this anymore."

But now Emily had second thoughts.

"Our adventure lasted a night and a day," she pointed out. "Maybe we should wait until morning after all."

They went to bed early, huddling together for comfort. They were chilled by their mother's offhand "Will? Oh, he's already gone to sleep, I expect."

They slept fitfully and woke at daybreak. They tiptoed barefoot to Will's room, hoping against hope to see his small shape curling the covers into a comma. But the bed was flat and empty, and scanning the garden from his window, they saw no shadow of a boy.

They couldn't wait any longer. Creeping out the back door, they made their way to the shrubbery of the secret passage. The book still lay there, held open by the low branches of the hawthorn bush.

"Will," Anne whispered, taking hold of one side.

"Will," Emily called softly, grasping the other.

They brought their hands together, snapping the book shut with a sound that echoed through the garden.

And there he was, sitting beside them, with a faraway look in his blue eyes.

Anne and Emily hugged and kissed him and asked him a torrent of questions. But he was unmoving in their arms and said nothing at all. His eyes, unfocused and unblinking, continued to watch something they couldn't see, as though he was awake but still dreaming.

Anne burst into tears. "I knew we shouldn't have done it," she cried. "He's not really here at all. Part of him stayed behind."

"Maybe he's just under a spell," Emily said hopefully.

Their mother's face appeared at her bedroom window. "For heaven's sake, children, it's five o'clock in the morning!" she said in an angry whisper. "Get back to bed this minute."

It was no easy task to get Will to bed. Finally Emily and Anne devised a shuffling sandwich method, with Emily in front, holding his arms over her shoulders, and

Anne propping him up from behind and pushing. The stairs were particularly gruesome going, and there was a bumpy part near their parents' bedroom that drew a groaning protest from their father: "Can't I even get a little peace in my own house in the middle of the night?"

Finally they dumped the glassy-eyed Will on his bed, and sank exhausted to the floor. Anne, who had managed to keep the book tucked under her arm during the whole operation, now dropped it alongside the pile of other books.

"That book is turning into a nightmare," said Emily, shaking her head at Will, who was staring unseeingly at the ceiling.

Anne hugged her knees and chewed the end of her braid fiercely.

"I think we're the problem," she said at last. "I mean, we tried to keep Will away from the book at first. Then when he found his own way in, we interfered. Probably the last thing he wanted was a botched rescue by a couple of big sisters. I think he's supposed to handle his adventure by himself. All we've done is complicate things and mess up the magic."

"You're probably right," Emily acknowledged. "But what can we do about it now?"

"Leave the book with him and go back to bed," said

Anne. "It's Saturday, and the parents will be sleeping late. If we're lucky, it'll straighten itself out before they get up. I sure hope so, because I have a strong hunch they'll notice now that he isn't all there instead of not being there at all, if you know what I mean."

But Emily stretched out on the rug beside Will's bed.

"I'll keep watch for a while," she said. "Just in case."

The truth was, she felt a mix of acute guilt and envy, and neither emotion would let her leave Will alone with the book. But it was dark in the room, and the sound of her brother's regular breathing was so soothing that she soon rested her cheek against one arm and closed her eyes.

A few minutes later, when the front cover of the book began to tremble, she was fast asleep.

✳

"Come on, *heave*, all of you. Put your shoulders into it," said a muffled voice. "Ow, not into *me*, you sniggle snort."

"Snort sniggle yourself," came the shrill retort. "You keep sliding back into me. Oh, help, there I go now. This is all so slippery."

"Catch my hand!" said a deeper voice, like the creak of an old floorboard. "There you are, now move over to the edge. Yes, Hackberry in the center with me. On the count of three, everybody push. One, two, three, *ooof!*"

If anyone had been watching from the shadows, they would have seen a small book on the floor shake and settle and shake again, until at last the top cover and half the pages were hoisted open from within. Four anxious little faces peered out, as though from a large storm cellar.

It was the Gnomblins, of course, but now the tallest was no bigger than Will's index finger—far too small to catch sight of him on the bed high above them.

"Strange territory," said Hackberry, eyeing the pile of books that rose jaggedly before them. "Mountainous, you could say."

"Must be something wrong with your eyes," countered Mockerskin, who was lifting the bottom edge of the front cover and looking out over an unbroken expanse of floor toward the pale glow of a distant window. "It's as flat as a pancake."

"You're both blind, is what I say," put in Spiderwort from the opposite edge, which had a good view under the bed. "It's an enormous dark tunnel, full of dandelion fluff and milkweed. Or is it a flock of sheep?"

"By all the runes," thundered Bullthistle, who shared Hackberry's perspective but had craned his neck enough to get a more complete view of their surroundings, "this is not a geographers' convention! Spiderwort, hop out and find something to prop this tome open before our strength gives out."

The skinniest Gnomblin slithered down and crept under the bed, searching the gloom for something more substantial than the dust balls he'd taken for dandelion fluff. He reemerged a minute later, sneezing and rolling a big, dusty lump of Play-Doh that had settled under Will's bed weeks before.

"How's this?" he asked excitedly. "Pretty good, don't you think? I was quick, wasn't I? Pretty good work, eh?"

"Oh, stop your silly chattering and lift it up to me," snapped Mockerskin. And with some grunting and griping, the Play-Doh was pushed into place so it held the book ajar.

The three other Gnomblins crawled out. They hesitated for a moment, standing close together in the vast, dusky space, listening. Far away, near the window, the surface of the floor had the faint shine of a pool of water in the night. But elsewhere the shadows were deep and looming. Suddenly the air echoed with an enormous sigh.

"What was that? Oh, what was that?" yelped Spiderwort, clutching Bullthistle's sleeve.

"Not the wind, I reckon," said Hackberry. "Something alive, I'd say."

"Well, t'ain't dead, that's for sure," rejoined Mocker-skin, and he snickered nervously as another sigh—or was it a snore?—reverberated through the air.

"Hush," whispered Bullthistle. "Pull yourselves to-gether. We must find Will. Let's climb the mountain for a good look round. He can't be far."

And they began clambering up the stack of books at Will's bedside, pushing and pulling one another until they reached the red plateau of *Compton's Encyclopedia*. They stood there, panting for breath.

It was Mockerskin who first realized that the lumpy landscape that now came into view, though still above their heads, was shaped like a human being. But he saw it the way you might spot a sailing ship or a dragon in the clouds on a summer day.

"Just like a knee there, isn't it?" he remarked. "And look, there's the shoulder."

Then the shoulder shifted slightly, and a head covered with straight, fair hair drooped against it.

"It's Will," shrieked Spiderwort, "and, and . . . he's GROWN!"

✳

In the gray darkness at the foot of the bed, half hidden by its bulk, Emily opened her eyes. The room looked strange to her from the floor. The night's shadows sifted into odd heaps in the corners as the faint morning light pressed in.

Her eyes sought the book, and she quickly recognized its spine a few feet from her face. But it was tilted, she thought, askew somehow. Then she heard the whispering, tiny but urgent.

"Will!" someone was calling. "Will!" And she saw them, four agitated little figures silhouetted atop a pile of books.

Later, she was very proud that she didn't scream. In fact, she stopped breathing for a second, and lay perfectly still. Fleetingly, she thought of *The Borrowers*, a book she had loved about little people who live under the floorboards of old houses. Then, as the four figures jostled one another, the pale gray light from the window briefly caught a face she recognized.

It was the little man in the picture, the one Will had followed. Now he was standing a little to one side. One of the others had backed to the edge of the broad book at the top of the stack. He ran forward, jumped, churned his small legs wildly in the air, and clutched hold of the bedsheet halfway down to the floor as the others cried out in their tinny, creaky little voices.

It was comical, but heroic, too, Emily thought. The one who'd jumped struggled up the sheet, hand over hand. He had almost made it when Will opened his eyes. Any remaining fears Emily harbored about these elfin men were put to rest in the next few minutes. She saw Will smile down as the first one hoisted himself over the top and helped the others up, one by one.

"The book," they cried to Will. "Get the book!" And careful not to dislodge them as they shrank against his pillow, Will reached down and plucked it from the floor.

Long afterwards, Emily remembered that last image: Will's face proud and happy as he turned the pages, and, in the half-light, the little men crowding close to see. Then she blinked, and they were all gone.

THE LAKE OF STONE SHORES

One moment Will had been sprinting across the last yards of the wasteland toward grass and earth and the rejoicing Gnomblins. The next moment, when Anne and Emily closed the book, he felt wrenched through space, as though he were being sucked unwillingly into wakefulness from a dream, or, rather, from an experience that would turn into a dream as soon as he gave up and let himself awaken. Instead he struggled, stubbornly refusing to let go.

In ordinary sleeping dreams, he'd never been able to stem the tide of wakefulness, however hard he'd tried. He still remembered one dream where he'd flown to a Christmas tree farm and found brightly wrapped presents growing in the glittering snow. He'd just begun harvesting the mysterious gifts, his red boots crunching deliciously through the snow crust, when his mother's voice penetrated the dream and dragged him up into a rainy school day.

This time, however, he hung on. It was as though he were trying to ignore an unruly audience while watching a movie unfold. Though he had a dim awareness of Anne and Emily, like obnoxious strangers beside him in a darkened theater, his attention was focused on the images flickering across the screen of his other consciousness.

He saw himself surrounded by the cheering Gnomblins, passing the pouch with its precious cargo to Bullthistle, who stroked his beard and smiled and nodded, and then looked questioningly into his eyes. Will tried to speak, but he wasn't sure whether the words explaining the riddle were only echoing in his own head.

It took all his strength to ignore the pushing and pulling of his body as Anne and Emily got him to bed.

Then he saw Bullthistle raise a honeysuckle tumbler filled with sweet water, and watched himself drink it down. But all the while his own great thirst remained unquenched.

He saw the Gnomblins' worried faces as they led him to a sheltered patch of moss. He sank into the soft green and immediately fell asleep.

Soon he began to dream that he was sleeping in his own bed at home. But in the dream something kept whispering and crackling nearby, until at last he opened his eyes and saw a small reddened hand clutching the sheet just over the edge of the mattress, and then Hackberry's broad, perspiring face pulled into view. Abruptly, it disappeared again. But in the dream it was tiny—hardly bigger than a pencil eraser.

All the other Gnomblins had shrunk, too. They stood on the pile of books by Will's bed, shouting encouragement and advice to Hackberry as he climbed up, hand over hand.

"That's it! Scrabble with your toes a bit."

"No, no, you're slipping again."

"Of course, he's slipping, you snerk—why'd you tell him to scrabble?"

And so on. It was a very amusing dream. At last Hackberry had hoisted himself onto the bed, and throwing himself on his stomach near the edge, he reached

down to pull the others up: first it was Spiderwort, hiccup-
ing with excitement as he dangled; then, with Spiderwort
sitting on Hackberry's legs as anchor, it was Mockerskin,
who bounced off the side of the bed each time Spiderwort
gave one of his high-pitched hiccups. And finally, with all
three helping, Bullthistle, who blew into his beard to keep
his dignity as he was dragged over the top.

Will had a good laugh later, telling the Gnomblins
about the dream over a late breakfast of raspberry juice
and pine nuts.

"You were all talking at the same time," he said, "but
finally I understood that you wanted me to pick up a book,
and it turned out to be that special book. I kept turning
the pages, and seeing the pictures of my own battles with
Forficula's squadrons, and pointing them out to you guys.
You were so small in the dream you could all crowd in at
the bottom of a page. Then I turned another page, and
there I was, sleeping on the moss. And then I woke up."

The Gnomblins eyed one another and smiled, and
were suddenly all very busy clearing away the breakfast
things.

They were camped at the edge of the great prairie, and
it hummed under the steady shine of the hot noonday
sun. Bullthistle had said Will must reach the Lake of
Stone Shores by midafternoon to complete the second

part of the quest. And there would be no time to return before heading for Break Neck Cliff, northwest of the lake, to get there before nightfall.

"You'll have to travel light," Hackberry told him. "No sword. No missiles and such."

All Will was given was a long-handled, finely woven butterfly net, and a kind of squirt gun fashioned from a hollow reed, with a quill nozzle and a wooden plunger. It was empty, but Mockerskin told him how to pull on the plunger to suck up water from the lake when he reached it, and how a sharp push would send a strong stream shooting out from the nozzle almost as far as an arrow. Finally, there was something to contain the object of the quest: a small golden flask, with a radiant sun etched into its golden stopper, and a pattern of stylized waves along the rounded sides.

" 'Too small to see, in death I live,' " Will muttered. "It should be easier to guess the second time around, but I just can't think of a watery answer to the same riddle. And I'll never make it to the lake before noon, even if the dragonflies don't get me. There must be acres and acres of prairie."

"Just hold on a minute," said Bullthistle. A smile hovered at the corners of his thin lips. "We've a way to give you some speed."

Then Mockerskin ducked into the shoulder-high grass and emerged a moment later leading something that glittered in a splendor of gold and green. Through the quickening of his own heartbeat, Will heard Bullthistle say, "This is your steed, Melanoplus."

It was a spur-throated grasshopper, big as a pony. Its head and thorax were burnished like yellow brass, its powerful hind legs marked with a feather pattern of greenish brown, just like Will's very favorite picture in his insect book. A grass-green harness circled its neck, and looped reins of the same stuff rested lightly on its back.

Will mounted easily, and, without a pause for goodbyes, they were off.

Up bounded the grasshopper, up, up toward the blue sky, and then down again, deep in the high grass, with Will barely clinging on, like a bronco rider in a rodeo.

"Grip with your knees!" shouted Mockerskin, who was now some distance away, barely visible through the thick screen of grasses.

"Hold tight to the reins," yelled Hackberry.

"Use your toes," shrilled Spiderwort.

Use your toes? But in fact, looking down, Will remembered he was barefoot, and by tucking his toes under Melanoplus and squeezing with his knees, he could keep his seat quite well through the grasshopper's roller-coaster leaps across the prairie.

It was a perfect July day. Will had never seen a sky so high and blue as the one he vaulted into each time Melanoplus bounded forward, through air that vibrated with sunlight and the song of crickets and katydids. Then came the downward swoop into stippled shadow, and the secret scurrying of the ants and leafhoppers that scrambled out of the way when he landed.

What a great way to travel, thought Will, as they skimmed under a startled tiger swallowtail, the scalloped edges of the butterfly's enormous velvet wings almost brushing his hair as they passed. Then the descent plunged them too close for comfort to a bright green creature with long, jagged, sickle-shaped jaws that gnashed at Will's toes as Melanoplus took off again.

"Whew, what a close shave," Will said, patting Melanoplus and looking back to see if the tiger beetle was pursuing them. "Good old Mel, you gave him the slip." And he was sure the grasshopper steed gave a modest wave of his antennae in reply before landing and leaping once more.

Soon Will realized they were approaching the lake. The butterflies were left behind, and the air was filled with the loud green buzz of green darners on patrol over their water territory. But when Melanoplus stopped just inside the end of the tall grass and Will saw the curved shoreline, he was astonished. It was like no lake he had ever seen.

The shore seemed like coarse sand at first glance, but when he dismounted and walked over, Will found it hard as stone, the pebble fragments embedded in flat rock. The curved edge fell away abruptly to where dark-green water lay, an arm's length lower down. Will's side of the lake seemed to be a great semicircle, but whether the other side completed the circle he couldn't tell. It was very far away. Will's view was obscured by a massive, towering object in the center. Dark, mottled gray-green, it loomed, not all of a piece but twisted into different shapes, ominously still.

Near the shore, the surface of the water rippled with life. Feathery-gilled naiads that would someday turn into gangly stone flies darted up from the depths, dimpling the water as they searched for gnats. A water strider as big as a life raft skated by. A kayak-shaped backswimmer churned the water with its oarlike hind legs.

A boat. Of course, that was what he needed, Will realized. Why hadn't he thought of it earlier? More to the point, why hadn't the Gnomblins included at least an inflatable raft when they'd outfitted him? Surely he wasn't expected to *swim* to the middle of the lake to find whatever-it-was, amid water insects made gigantic by Forficula's growth curse, not to mention to "fight where the water flows," as the rune put it.

Feeling hot and cross, Will looked back at Melanoplus, browsing in the deep grass. A grasshopper wasn't going to be any help here, he decided.

"Wait for me there, Mel, old boy," he said. And he began casting about the shore for material to make a raft.

He was ready to give up when he spotted a slender, long-legged insect using its forelegs to layer two leaves over some bobbing twig debris in the water. It was a water boatman (family *Corixidae*). Poor swimmers, these creatures actually made themselves crafts out of flotsam and jetsam and piloted them over ponds to hunt aquatic insects and stranded gnats. The leaf vessel was as big as a good-sized rowboat, Will judged—large enough, surely, for a passenger, as long as the boatman didn't mistake him for a meal.

"Uh, hi there," he called down. "Could you give me a ride?"

But the startled insect abandoned ship with one leap and disappeared.

"Oh, well, thanks for the boat," Will murmured, snagging it with the long handle of his net and drawing it alongside the edge, just below him. "Here goes."

And he jumped as lightly as he could onto the concave surface of the leaf craft.

It rocked perilously under his feet, and water pooled over the lowest edge. But sitting cross-legged in the center, he was able to steady the boat. He unslung his reed squirt gun and used it to bail out, suctioning up the water and spewing it over the side.

He found he could paddle pretty well with his hands, and the splashing noise seemed to frighten off the other water insects. He stretched his legs out, feeling the sun warm on his back and the delicious cool of the water flowing under him. He felt so lazy and untroubled for a time that when the surface of the water began to wrinkle more deeply beyond the boat's prow, he watched the ripples idly at first.

For a moment he thought he saw the reflection of a huge, dark face. Then the image was dissolved by ripples, and all at once he heard the sound of running water. And he realized with a jolt of fear that his boat was caught in a powerful current.

It spun out of control, dipping and dancing on the waves. Will had to grab a stem at the stern to keep himself from sliding off. Heartsick, he saw his net slip off the edge and start to sink. He reached into the water for it, but the wet netting slipped through his fingers as the boat careened away. Just when he thought he had lost the net for good, the vortex swept it back into the path of the leaf vessel, and Will wrenched it back from the water.

But the effort cost the boat the last of its balance. Will barely had time to sling the net on his shoulder with his water gun before the craft capsized. Down he went, sucked under by the whirlpool of the sinking boat.

The water was cold over his head. His feet stretched down without feeling bottom. Kicking against the dark, he burst into sunshine again, spluttering and blinking.

The rainbow blur of a dragonfly's wings swooped at his head, grinding the air like a chainsaw, and Will ducked down once more. Now that he was struggling in the water, he'd become fair game to the winged predators of the pond, he realized.

He held his breath, opened his eyes, and peered through the murky water. He was a good swimmer for his age, after Tiny Tadpole lessons as a baby and a Red Cross course last spring. But dodging flying bugs the size of helicopters had definitely not been part of his training at the Y.

Which way to swim? He had lost all sense of direction. He could only turn slowly underwater, seeking the shallows. Then, only a few yards away, he saw something dark and solid that seemed to extend all the way down to the unseen bottom. He struck out for it underwater, kicking hard.

It was part of the massive object in the center of the lake, he realized, as he clung to the cold, slippery sides and came up for air. He dragged himself out. He was perched on a dark metal surface, hot with the sun, just above the water. Panting, he glanced up, and went cold with terror. Right above him, seemingly suspended in the air, was a giant metal foot.

He cringed, then stared. It was immobile. Mottled gray and green, it was bigger than he was, but a foot just the same. He could see the bare toes, plump, pudgy ones, turned down toward the water. And yes, if he craned back his head and squinted against the afternoon sun, he could see the leg attached to it, rising up to join a dark, towering mass that had to be the rest of the body. That was much too high for Will to make out clearly.

He suddenly remembered a class trip to the Statue of Liberty. This, too, was an enormous statue. Scanning the top of the base onto which he had climbed, he now saw the thick metal shaft that held it up, running behind another foot and leg.

For the first time since he'd found himself in Jardinia,

Will felt profoundly uneasy. He'd been frightened before—panic-stricken, really, when the giant moths attacked, for instance, and later, when Death Mountain split open. But this was different: a deep-down, nameless anxiety that made his skin feel tight and strange, as though it no longer fit him.

Something didn't fit. Forficula's spell might have power over living things, and perhaps, in a way, over the dead, he thought. But not over tarnished metal. Yet surely this monstrous thing was not its true size, notwithstanding the Statue of Liberty.

He looked down at his own feet, wet and pale against the metal base of the statue. They looked very small. No bigger than a bug's, he thought suddenly.

Then something flashed bright orange in the dark water below him, and a huge, carrot-colored fish slipped to the surface, mouthed at him, and flicked away again.

It was like a warning. On instinct, Will grabbed his reed gun and knelt to fill it from the lake. The air began to vibrate and whine, to thicken, to swarm. He was engulfed, unable to see or breathe through the cloud of beating wings as thousands of small creatures rose from the surface of the water and surrounded him.

Blindly, he shot out a jet of water from the squirt gun, and some of the insects faltered and fell. But others took their place. Wailing, they rose and dropped about him as he tried to fight them off with his beating arms.

It was no use. He coughed and choked and spit. They were in his eyes, his nose, his throat, wave upon frenzied wave. Desperate, he unslung his butterfly net. On a sudden wave of inspiration, he popped it over his own head. It served as a kind of mosquito netting, he found, providing him breathing room amid the swarm.

As he watched through the fine mesh, he realized that the insects weren't mosquitoes hungry for his blood. They were mayflies in a mating swarm, little insects who ate nothing, mated, laid tiny eggs in the water, and died the same day.

"Order *Ephemeroptera*," Will's father had labeled them. "Like the word *ephemeral*. That's Latin for something that doesn't last. Here today and gone tomorrow."

"But what's the point?" Will had asked. "They don't even get to see their babies."

His father had sighed and taken off his reading glasses. "I guess it's the circle of life, pared down and speeded up. The eggs hatch into naiads, and the naiads eat pond debris. I suppose that does some greater good—keeping the water clean, you know. Then they grow up and molt into mayflies, and start the whole thing all over again in their one day of adult life."

His father had closed the insect book abruptly and tousled Will's hair. "Don't worry about it, old buddy," he'd said. "Just be glad you're not a midge or a mayfly. Our own life circle has a little more room to maneuver. Now, how about a game of catch before it gets too dark or my office calls?"

The circle of life, Will thought. Another circle that answers the riddle.

And then the mayflies veered away from him, onto the lake, to lay eggs too small to see.

Will was leaning out to look after them when a big brass-colored body hurtled down beside him. A glossy black eye looked at him quizzically through the butterfly net.

"Melanoplus!" he cried, tears of relief welling in his eyes. "My own true steed. How on earth did you get here?"

He could have sworn the spur-throated grasshopper shrugged his antennae, as if to say, "Oh, it was nothing."

Obviously, Will had underestimated Melanoplus's leaping ability, to say nothing of his courage. Given a floating leaf here and there to spring from, Mel was better than a boat, Will decided.

"Just a minute, old boy," he told the steed. And reaching out as far as he dared, he filled his squirt gun carefully from the surface of the water. He squeezed the water into the little golden flask the Gnomblins had given him.

"There's got to be at least one mayfly egg in there now," he told himself, twisting in the stopper and stowing it back in the pouch at his belt. "Now, let's get out of here!"

As the grasshopper soared out over the other side of the lake, making for a lily pad the size of an aircraft carrier, Will gave a backward glance at the statue that still haunted him. But all he saw was a dark presence through a blur of falling water.

And then they were deep in the grass again, heading for Break Neck Cliff.

TOO SMALL TO SEE

Emily didn't move for several seconds after Will vanished. Then, very slowly, she walked to his empty bed, picked up the open book, and began to read the picture story of Will's quest to Death Mountain.

"I'm sure the elf guys are okay," she told Anne later, after recounting the story of the little men who had appeared at Will's bedside. "Just look at the pictures, and you can tell they're the good guys. Will is helping them, the way we helped Robin Hood rescue Will Scarlet. I just know he'll be back tonight."

"I still wish you'd woken me up," Anne said for the tenth time. "I would have liked to see them, too, you know."

"I told you, there was no way to even move without scaring them away," Emily replied, holding her exasperation in check. "Look, let's just leave the book on Will's bed and spend the day doing peaceful, ordinary Saturday things, and not even think about magic. Okay?"

And that's what they did.

Anne drove with her still unnoticing father to the farmers' market, and they came back laden with strawberries and nectarines, tender red leaf lettuce, crisp green beans, and little russet potatoes. He had consulted with her over every purchase, and she felt wise and generous as she heaped the bounty of summer onto the kitchen table. Emily stayed behind to help her still unnoticing mother bake shortcake from scratch and mix the ultimate vinaigrette dressing, with lots of garlic and crushed basil from the garden.

They had the perfect summer lunch on the front porch—*salade niçoise*, fresh bread, and strawberry shortcake for dessert—with the opera *Don Giovanni* playing too loudly from the living room. The office didn't even call until the last crumb had been eaten.

In the afternoon, Anne and Emily fell back on the half-forgotten pastimes of early childhood, pulling out old paint sets and plasticine from a back shelf, and even, from the depths of their closet, a battered cardboard box that Emily had made into a haunted dollhouse last Halloween.

They revived the haunted box with spooky tinfoil mirrors, real cobwebs, and a pool of scarlet vermilion blood. They even disguised an old Ginny doll as Dracula.

"If only we could show Will," said Anne, voicing Emily's thought exactly. "Let's swear an oath right now that if there's another adventure to be had out of that book, we three do it together. No more of this traipsing off by yourself. I never thought I could miss him so much."

Later, they caught their mother by surprise as she came in with a basket of clean laundry, and begged her to read aloud to them, as she used to do when they were small.

"Read 'Jack and the Beanstalk,' " said Emily. And in a whisper she added, "Will's favorite."

"And read it in Will's room," Anne urged.

"Well, all right," their mother said. "But first help me fold everything and put the clothes away."

It was almost evening when they sat down together on Will's bed, after moving the magic book to the windowsill, propped open. Anne and Emily leaned close to their mother as she read aloud, her voice a little husky, her skin smelling faintly of geraniums. Outside, the sunlight slanted, reddened, gradually faded. Passing by the room, their father stopped and lingered in the doorway, caught by the old words and the picture mother and daughters made together.

"You don't have enough light," he said. And leaning down, he switched on a lamp against the dusk.

※

All along, as Melanoplus bounded uphill, Will was bracing himself for the moment when the grasshopper steed would suddenly halt, and the earth would fall away before them. He was hoping he wouldn't get sick looking down, the way he had on the amusement park Ferris wheel at Jeremy Belmont's birthday party. *Break Neck Cliff.* Well, at least it wouldn't go round and round, he thought.

He was completely unprepared for the sheer cliff wall that rose abruptly before him as they emerged from thick underbrush. It was rough brown in the fading light, with no sign of a foothold, no glimpse of the top.

" 'Climb high and see as do the crows,' " he muttered,

repeating the words of the rune. "That's just plain ridiculous, unless I can fly like a crow, too."

He gave a halfhearted wave of his arms, to no effect. Dismounting, he began to walk along the bottom of the cliff, looking for a way up.

Before long, his way was blocked by a thick green vine that twined up against the cliffside, as high as the eye could see. The leaves were as big as Will, and the stems thicker than tree limbs.

"I've always wondered what it would be like to climb a magic beanstalk," he told himself. "I guess this is my chance to find out."

And leaving net, gun, and flask with Melanoplus, he scrambled into the vine.

Almost as easy as climbing stairs, it was, the branches firm and steady under his bare feet, the handholds plentiful along the way. Up and up he climbed, face to the cliff—not scared, but not daring to turn and look down.

He was already quite high when he began to think of the ogre in the story. An ugly brute in the picture book Will knew so well, with jagged teeth and clawlike fingernails and hobnail boots, the better to grind your bones.

Fi-fie-fo-fum, I smell the blood of an Englishman. Maybe the ogre was saying it already, hairy nostrils to the evening breeze, with an evil glint in his squinty eyes and drool dribbling down the mole on his chin.

"Hey, big guy, I'm American," Will muttered defensively. But the ogre in his mind's eye didn't seem deterred by a mere question of nationality. Will paused, panting, and considered climbing down again.

It was getting late. He had only until nightfall to complete the last part of the quest, and if he turned back now, he might not have another chance. Besides, he thought, if he was standing in for Jack, it should come out right in the end. He started climbing again.

Higher and higher he went. He came to a place where the cliff seemed to jut out in a ledge above his head. *Perhaps I'm coming close to the end here*, he thought. He scrambled up onto the ledge, turning as he did so. And with one arm hooked around the vine for support, he looked down.

Like a book, the landscape opened to his eyes. The glint of water to the right. The long stretch of grass rolling down. Gray stone under a canopy of shadow. In the last light of the long day, Will saw Jardinia, and knew it for his own garden.

He felt himself sway, dizzy with recognition. The lake was his mother's round goldfish pond, with its fountain statue of a boy holding a dolphin. The wasteland was the flagstone floor of the wisteria arbor. And Death Mountain, as he had half guessed, was a compost heap—the very one he'd fed himself sometimes, with banana peels and apple cores.

He'd been too close before, too small to see the garden for the grass.

Too small to see.

The thought caught him in the chest like a blow. It was he who had shrunk, not the garden and its inhabitants who had grown, whatever the Gnomblins believed—or pretended to believe. He now remembered certain looks they'd exchanged, certain phrases. They had held something back.

Too small to see.

Was he himself the last piece of the riddle, then? He took a deep breath, trying to steady himself. The rest of the riddle's words echoed in his mind, mixed up with dimly remembered phrases from his Grandfather Thornton's funeral.

"In the midst of life, we are in death . . . A time to be born, and a time to die . . ."

It was too much to grasp, too big for him. And yet, with a certainty that filled his lungs like air, he knew it was true.

Below him, twilight settled on the garden, and the first fireflies flickered. Behind him, the glow of a lamp suddenly shone out on the ledge that was his own windowsill.

He turned and saw them then: his mother, dark hair shining in the lamplight, book open on her lap; his sisters, leaning, with upturned faces, into the curve of her arms; his father, resting one hand lightly on her shoulder, and bending to see the page.

Leaning forward with longing, he saw the same picture, repeated small and bright like a reflection in the pupil of an eye. It was on the open pages of the magic book, which lay over the threshold of the dark window frame, on the inner sill.

And then he fell.

＊

" 'But Jack jumped down and got hold of the axe and gave a chop at the beanstalk,' " Will's mother was reading. " 'The ogre felt the beanstalk shake and quiver.' "

And Will was right there in her lap, with Anne and Emily on either side and his father close by, and "Jack and the Beanstalk" open to the last two pages.

Will saw the words as his mother read them. For the first time, the letters didn't crowd his field of vision and overwhelm him. It was as though he saw them from a distance, from far away enough to recognize the patterns they made, like a landscape revealed from a great height. There was *axe* and *shake*, and farther down the page, where his mother's voice had not yet traveled, *they lived happy ever after*.

He could read.

✳

"But what about the Gnomblins?" Emily asked after Will had told them everything, which was not until fairly late the next day, after the happiness of being a whole family had almost settled into a regular Sunday feeling again, and the three children had crept off to Will's room for a conference. "What about Forficula's spell?"

"It's broken, of course—anyone can see that," said Anne, with a toss of her braids.

Emily looked doubtful. "But what about mixing the grass and the water, potionlike. Bubble, bubble, toil and trouble, hocus-pocus, and all that?"

"That's silly," snapped Anne, who was still slightly out of sorts because she had been left out of the adventure. Emily, after all, had at least seen the Gnomblins. "The third thing couldn't have been mixed in a potion, anyway. It was knowledge, sort of, that came from climbing high up and recognizing the garden. The point is, Will followed the rune and did the three quests, right? And besides, maybe the spell was really about shrinking Will, not making everything else grow, so it would have been broken anyway when he came back through the book, I bet."

Anne and Emily argued about that for a while. Then they argued about whether, if they had looked in the right places in the garden at the right times, they would have found their brother, only tiny, and whether the Gnom-blins existed only in the book or all the time, "like Bor-rowers, only different," as Emily put it.

"What do you think, Will?" asked Anne at last.

"Yes, Will, what do you think?" asked Emily.

"Huh?" remarked Will, looking up from the midst of books scattered far and wide over his floor. "Could you please keep it down? I'm reading."

GARDEN PARTY

It was late August. All night the heat had lingered in the upstairs bedrooms of the house. At daybreak, no breeze stirred the curtains at Anne and Emily's windows. As the sun rose, a stifling, humid haze oppressed the garden, too.

All Anne wanted to do when she woke was to lie on top of the sheets in the path of the electric fan, staring at the ceiling: so white, so cool, like an expanse of new-fallen snow.

When Anne was younger she had made a game of imagining life on the high ceilings of the house. Their clean, bare surfaces were especially inviting in hot weather. Then life below seemed choked by overstuffed chairs, magazine racks crammed tight with newspapers, mantels crowded with her parents' souvenirs. She would imagine escaping to the upside-down image of the cluttered rooms, gliding in spaces made vast by emptiness. Up there it was always winter, she thought—not the real winter that arrived in bits and pieces, in cold rain and muddy days, but the winter one suddenly longed for in the middle of a heat wave.

Her daydream was interrupted by her parents' voices in the hall.

"Who in their right mind gives a garden party in August?" her father was grumbling. "The hottest day of the year, no less."

"Now, darling, you know it's practically a *Daily Herald* tradition," her mother replied in a soothing tone as they descended the stairs. "Last year the weather cooperated beautifully. Maybe we'll still get a quick rainstorm to clear the air before evening."

Anne's heart sank. Somehow she had forgotten that

her parents' annual garden party was tonight. Any moment she and Emily would be sucked into the frantic preparations. Sure enough, their father began calling their names in accents of outrage as soon as he reached the living room. He had just encountered the scattered pieces of half a dozen board games, Anne realized.

They had tried to combine the games into a super-spectacular version of their own invention. It was shaping up quite nicely, too, until Will lost his temper over rules that kept changing and knocked every last piece to the floor. Everybody had stalked or flounced out in a different direction, leaving the grand experiment all over the Oriental rug.

For days on end, the three children had been trying to stay together as much as possible and to keep the book within easy reach. This time, when—or if—another magic adventure beckoned, they had vowed not to be separated.

For a while it was fun. There was a family picnic at Jones Beach one weekend, with the book stashed in a plastic bag in Will's backpack, just in case, and the three children sharing sandy peanut butter sandwiches and jumping endless waves. There were uneventful excursions to the local swimming pool, with spluttery games of "swimming machine," an invention of Emily's that called for the bigger child to paddle madly while the smaller one held on to her waist and kicked, trying (and always failing) to keep them both afloat. And there were the times when they simply read the best nonmagic books around, mostly in companionable silence, except when Will insisted on reading his favorite parts of *The Moffats* out loud, even though Emily was deep in the world of the Melendy family, and Anne was struggling with the dauntingly thick novel by Tolstoy that she had borrowed in defiance of the librarian's skeptical look.

"*War and Peace?*" her father said incredulously, looking over her shoulder just when she was guiltily skipping to the last pages, trying to figure out what happened to Natasha in the end. "Don't rush it, kiddo. Like most of life's good things, it's worth waiting for."

But as August grew unbearably hot and the magic book's pages stayed stubbornly shut, all that waiting and togetherness had begun to drive them crazy. Lately, every distraction they tried seemed to end in a messy squabble.

One day they played at being alchemists, turning dross into gold with the help of a can of yellow paint and a small jar of glitter. Who could have guessed that some dusty old glass paperweight wasn't dross to their father, or that it would take them hours to scrape out the glitter that stuck in that inscription they had overlooked, "From your admiring colleagues at *The Rutland Post-Gazette*"?

Another time they made a tent over the clothesline, using bedspreads and croquet hoops, and Anne was the Gypsy fortune-teller who said, "Cross my palm with silver." Who could have predicted that it would start raining hard just as Will and Emily collected nickels from the four Olandorf grandchildren, or that after their muddy stampede for shelter, the bedspreads would never be the same?

"This house is a disaster area," their father groaned from downstairs. "How are we ever going be ready by five o'clock?"

"Children!" their mother called. "All hands on deck!"

❋

For the next few hours, frenzied pickup and cleaning prevailed. Later there were deliveries to unpack, and last-minute trips to the store, prompted by the kind of questions the children had learned to dread, like "Can that really be the last of the sour cream?" and "What on earth happened to all those olives I bought last week?" Finally, after a period of panting collapse and the slurping of cold drinks, the battlefield shifted to the sultry garden.

Their mother clipped and tweaked vines, her face dirt-streaked and determined. Their father, balanced on a ladder under the wisteria arbor, cursed the tangle of electric wires he was supposed to weave through the foliage. The children gathered the odds and ends that had washed up on the patio over the summer—a battered badminton racket; the odd croquet hoop; a garlic press that had been used to mash leaves into the kind of poultice that might heal a wounded knight. When the kitchen phone rang, the only one close enough to answer it was Will.

The receiver crackled and sputtered at him. A woman's voice said, "Hold for long distance, please," and at last a man's shout broke through the static: "Hello, Thornton? Thornton? For godsake, kid, get him to the phone. Tell him it's an emergency. Tell him the cold war is getting hotter."

As soon as Will delivered the message, his father jumped off the ladder and ran inside. He began pacing back and forth as he listened, absentmindedly twirling the last strand of lights faster and faster until Will was sure a tray of waiting cocktail glasses was done for.

"Take it easy, Gordon," his father kept saying. "When did you last see Donderberg? And where was that, exactly? Wait a minute, isn't that in northern Transylvania? I thought we agreed you two would stay in Hungary. Okay, okay. Take it easy, Gordon. Cold war maneuvers may have nothing to do with it. Tell me everything, slowly, from the top."

He grabbed a pencil from the old marmalade jar near the sink and began scribbling on the nearest piece of paper. It was Aunt Nora's recipe for crabmeat canapés, Will noticed.

Cold war. This was getting exciting, Will thought. The words made him think of a snowball fight waged from ice forts behind deep drifts of snow. At the moment, Will was wedged between the broom closet and the oven, where his mother's puff pastry was baking, feeling as hot and sticky as he'd ever been in his life. But his father's words brought back the winter afternoon when he and his friend Aaron had talked of storing snowballs in the freezer. They'd given up too easily. How great would that be, to have a snowball fight on the hottest day in August!

"Just sit tight, Gordon," his father was saying. "Get some sleep, and stay away from the Russians. Maybe it's just a big misunderstanding. I'll make some calls and we'll talk in the morning." After some other reassuring words, he hung up.

By then the others had gathered in the kitchen to see what was afoot. Anne, Emily, and Will saw their parents' eyes meet, and recognized the let's-keep-calm-in-front-of-the-children look.

"Elizabeth, I've got a crisis," their father said quietly. "Nothing to worry about, kids," he added over his shoulder as he and their mother headed upstairs to the study to talk in private. "Just office stuff. Carry on."

Carry on? Honestly, parents were maddening, Emily thought. A huge bag of ice was melting in the sink. In the oven, the puff pastry was starting to singe. Anyone could see something enormous and unexpected had sliced through the summer afternoon, making even their father forget the imminent arrival of hordes of guests.

"Stay away from the Russians," Emily said, repeating what she had heard when she walked in. It made her think of the stories her mother sometimes told, family lore about the time Nana Baumgarten hid from marauding Cossacks in a snowdrift. In her mind's eye, Emily saw mustachioed men with fur hats flourishing whips as they drove their horses across a snowy landscape. She felt a delicious shiver of excitement.

Anne, having seen the serious look on her father's face, mainly felt worried. To her, the phrase "Stay away from the Russians" brought to mind school drills where the children had to practice taking shelter under their desks. ("Absurd," their father had once commented when she described them. "As though ducking under a desk could protect anyone from a nuclear bomb." Then, seeing her anxious face, he had tugged one of her braids and added, "No fear, sweetheart—it won't happen.")

But after pumping Will for more information, Anne grew skeptical.

"Transylvania? As in Dracula? Maybe it just sounded like that, Will," she suggested, trying to be diplomatic. "Some Russian place-name, probably. I'm pretty sure Gordon is that photographer in the Moscow bureau that Dad calls excitable."

The telephone rang again. This time, Anne grabbed it, but her father had already picked up the extension in his study.

"Donderberg, where the hell are you?" she heard him say over the static.

The answer was garbled by echoes on the line, but she could have sworn she heard the words *castle* and *Transylvania*.

"Is someone else on the line?" her father asked. "Hang up down there."

When their mother reappeared, the children were in a huddle, discussing vampires. She shooed them away to take showers and dress for the party.

"You've been watching too many old movies," she said. "Transylvania is actually just a wooded region in Romania, near the Hungarian border. *Sylvania* means 'forest' in Latin. Anyway, it seems it was all a mistake, just a reporter who missed his train connection or something. Your father will have it cleared up before the—oh, no," she broke off. "The pastry!"

And she lunged for the oven, waving a pot holder at the billowing smoke.

✳

A mix of relief and disappointment left Anne feeling even more lethargic. She was the last to shower in the puddled, steamy bathroom. Still damp, she lay on her bed to catch a moment of coolness before the day's accumulated heat pressed in on her again. In the open closet she saw her new dress waiting, a sleeveless sheath of summer green. In the store, it had made her think of Maid Marian moving with effortless grace through the banquet hall. But now she was sure it would crease in all the wrong places. Sweat and the unfamiliar swellings of her body would ruin the whole effect.

She heard the first guests arriving downstairs. Emily and Will were probably already passing out canapés. But still she lingered, watching the chilly shadows on the high white ceiling, wishing that she could spend the evening up there, skating from window to window.

By the time she pulled herself together, she could hear

that the party was in full swing. A jazzy song flowed under ripples of talk and laughter and tinkling glassware. The tune was one that her parents sometimes danced to. Suddenly they would glide in giddy embrace over the kitchen floor, regardless of the earth stains on her mother's gardening pants or her father's droopy cardigan. *What do I care how much it may storm? / I've got my love to keep me warm.* Straining to hear the words, Anne leaned out the window on the landing and saw the garden completely transformed.

The wisteria arbor was like a twinkling canopy of fallen stars. Tendrils of little lights ran up toward the house, and moonflower vines glowed white through the dusk. The guests eddied in the landscape, the women's bright dresses glimmering when they caught the light, the men's pale shirts almost phosphorescent. A woman with a pealing laugh and orange hair had taken off her high-heeled sandals and was dipping her bare feet into the gleaming pond.

"Ooh, the goldfish tickle," she squealed, loudly enough to be heard over the Billie Holiday song wafting through the French doors to the patio. *What do I care if icicles form? / I've got my love to keep me warm.*

For people in the garden, Anne realized, the party itself had turned the sullen heat of this August evening into a warm embrace. Part of her longed to belong down there, grownup, too, and swaying to the music. Part of her longed instead to be as indifferent as her six-year-old self, skipping through the guests without caring how she looked. This summer, she seemed caught somewhere in between. Maybe that was why she had been left out when Will and Emily saw Jardinia's inhabitants, she thought. Maybe she was growing too old for that kind of magic, even though she still had no place in the kind of magic that filled the garden now.

She was about to turn away when her eye was caught by a movement in the shadows at the bottom of the garden. And as she watched in astonishment, a dark, heavily wrapped figure emerged from the pines.

It paused, seeming to stretch taller in the dusk. There was something odd about the way it turned from side to side, almost as though trying to catch a scent in the air— like an animal, Anne thought, with a prickling at the back of her neck. The figure edged up the hill, keeping to the shrubbery until it had reached the thickest part of the crowd. Just as it melted into the throng, Anne had a glimpse of a thin, bearded face and an overcoat with a large fur collar.

Who on earth would wear a coat to a garden party in August? This was not some random guest returning from a solitary tour of her mother's garden, she thought. This was an interloper from somewhere else entirely. And she was certain he was up to no good. Without even stopping to glance in the mirror, Anne dashed down the stairs to find out.

THE BEARDED INTERLOPER

The kitchen was the shortest way to the garden. But now it was jammed with guests, and as Anne tried to make her way past knots of lively conversation and arms reaching into the refrigerator, her mother spotted her.

"Oh, Anne, there you are," she exclaimed, thrusting out a platter of crackers spread with goat cheese. "Please pass this around the patio. I have to deal with the ratatouille."

Well, perhaps canapé duty wasn't such a bad way to hunt down the mystery interloper, Anne thought, plunging through the crowd and out the back door with the platter held high. She moved as fast as she could, barely pausing long enough for people to snatch a cracker as she scanned their faces for beards. Outside, a man with a goatee caught her eye for a moment, but he was short and plump.

"When I teach *War and Peace,* I tell my students to read *between* the chapters," he was telling a woman draped in a shimmering fringed shawl. "Of course," he added, pausing for a triumphant chortle, "of course they *can't do it!*"

How mean! Anne thought, swinging the tray out of his reach. Who could possibly read the blank spaces between the chapters of a book? Or was that just an expression, like "reading between the lines"? The remark stirred something in her memory, something she knew she should not have forgotten, but before she could puzzle it out, another conversation caught her ear.

"Hey, did you see that guy in fur?" a woman was asking. "Where does Thornton find these people?"

"One of the new copy editors, I bet," her companion said. "That's the foreign desk for you."

Anne turned sharply, sending most of the crackers skidding. "Which way did he go?" she asked. "Did he have a beard?"

"Whoa, there!" the woman said, steadying the platter. "I wouldn't mind eating one of those. You're a Thornton, aren't you? I'm Alicia Freese, from metro. Now, what did you want to know?"

By the time Anne could confirm a beard and a general direction, she had missed her quarry. A young man in blue jeans and a paint-spattered shirt tried to be helpful.

"The overdressed fellow with the wolfish look? I think he went inside to ditch the coat. Is he that visiting art critic your mother mentioned?"

"*Homo homini lupus*," put in a pale young woman in black, whose beaded earrings dangled nearly to her bare shoulders. "Or, for those who have forgotten their Latin, *Every man is a wolf to every other man*. Actually," she added, draping an arm around the young man's waist, "I think your wolfman is one of Baumgarten's eccentric botanists. She collects them."

Anne didn't wait to discuss the question. Dropping the platter behind an azalea, she ran back into the house from the patio through the open French windows.

No sign of him in the dining room, where dance music now blared from floor speakers on either side of the buffet. No sign in the living room, where the plumped-up cushions and polished surfaces were still pristine. But craning her neck at the foot of the staircase, Anne thought she caught a glimpse of a long, dark coat on the second-floor landing.

The coat was draped over the banister, its fur collar still swaying slightly, like a wild creature waiting to spring. In the airless upstairs hallway, all the doors were shut. Anne hesitated for a moment outside her parents' bedroom, remembering that her mother kept jewelry in a sock drawer to fool would-be burglars. But this intruder was surely not after a pearl necklace, she thought. She hurried on, past Will's room, with its hand-lettered DO NOT DISTERB sign, past the silent bathroom, straight to her father's study, where she put her ear to the door. In the pause between two sambas, she heard the unmistakable creak of the floorboards inside. As quietly as possible, she turned the knob and pushed.

Sometimes within the family, they called the room the library. It had floor-to-ceiling bookshelves on three sides, an inviting window seat, and a floor lamp that cast a warm amber light. In the lamp's glow Anne now saw a dark figure in an ill-fitting worsted wool suit, stooped over something that held his avid attention. He was pawing at it with a kind of relish, his curved fingernails protruding from fingerless gloves. A muttering, guttural, growling sound suddenly came from his throat, and she found herself thinking of a ravenous animal that was about to eat.

Then he looked up, and in the same moment, Anne realized what he was holding.

The book! Somehow, in the frenzied picking up before the party, it had been collected and shelved here by mistake. How could they have been so careless? This was what the intruder had come for, and now he had it.

"That's our book," Anne declared, sounding more high-pitched than she wanted to as she met his eyes. They glittered almost yellow above a pointed dark beard and curling mustache.

"This book is not for children," he said in a whispery, rasping voice, gripping the volume to his chest. "The *Otiyot Hermetica* contains the secrets of dominion over time and earth, over wind and water—the most powerful magic of generations. It does not belong in this world at all. It is not to be trifled with."

"We're not trifling with it," Anne protested, reaching out for the book, which the intruder, she noticed, was holding the wrong way around. "And besides, it's—it's none of your business."

He laughed unpleasantly, showing long teeth. "My, my, we're quite the bold child, aren't we?" he said, tightening his grip. "Remember, young lady, a little knowledge is a dangerous thing."

And holding the book firmly in both hands, he opened it and turned away.

"Will! Emily!" Anne shouted, grabbing his coattails. "Quick! Quick! He's going to get away!"

Down she plunged, from the stifling August heat of the library through cold, white, whistling air, calling to her brother and sister and clinging to the rough wool of the intruder's jacket. It was all she could do to hang on in that rush of wind and whiteness. But if she let go, she knew, the book would be gone forever. Worse, its power would be turned to the service of this stranger and the evil hunger glittering in his yellow eyes.

He was taking the book with him even as he entered its pages, she realized. He was mastering the magic in a way they had never even tried. She still saw the book in her mind's eye, opening upside down in his hands to a blank page. Then that blankness seemed to envelope her, and she was falling, falling, falling, into an endless expanse of snow.

WINTER MASQUERADE

*T*here was a faint jingling of sleigh bells. The sound came from very far away, Anne thought dreamily. It was carried like starlight through dark, clear air. She stirred, and felt the sound explode in little starbursts of pins and needles. Better to lie still in the dark and sleep.

"Wake up, we're here," a girl's voice insisted. "Just look how lovely the house is tonight."

186

She opened her eyes and saw the silver roof of a great house in the moonlight. Icicles sparkled under the eaves, and candles glowed in every window. Little dogs barked and a door opened, spilling the glitter of diamonds and bluish shadows across the snow.

"*Who is it?" asked someone from the porch.*

"*The mummers from the count's. I know by the horses," other voices replied.*

There was laughter, shouting, and bits of song, and then the sound of boots scrunching on dry snow. Wrapped in a fur cloak, Anne did not feel the cold except in the sting of the frosty air in her nose, and the steam of her own breath when she exhaled. She looked at the girl who had wakened her and saw a face that was almost her own, yet different—laughing, rosy, with a funny charcoal mustache on her upper lip and curlicue charcoal eyebrows. Then they were engulfed by a merrymaking crowd carrying candles, and propelled into the house together.

It was the winter masquerade at the Melyukovs'. Hussars, fine ladies, witches, clowns, and bears stamped their feet, shed their cloaks, and moved into a candlelit ballroom as little children screamed for joy at their heels. The waltzing began, and before Anne could get her bearings, she was spinning in the arms of a handsome bear. Around the room she twirled, nearly brushing a great Christmas tree that glistened with sugar plums, candied orange slices, and twinkling silver nests of chocolate truffles. She could smell fir needles and nutmeg and a slight tang of peppermint.

"The hussar! The hussar!" different voices were saying. "And look how she dances!" Surely their eyes were on *her*. Yes, when she caught sight of herself in a mirror she saw a slim young girl in the close-fitting gold braid of a Russian cavalry hussar's uniform, her pretty face flushed, the smudge of her charcoal mustache stretched by a smile of pure happiness.

She remembered another waltz now, too. A grander ballroom lit by hundreds of candles, full of flowers and music and all the bright young people of St. Petersburg. Another mirror, where she could see herself with a rose in her dark hair, in a gauzy white dress over pink silk. It was her first ball, and she was gliding straight from the despair of longing to dance and being left out to the rapture of dancing all night and loving everything and everybody.

Into what box of delights had she stumbled? Dimly she recalled the fat volume of Tolstoy's *War and Peace* as it had nestled in the green hammock on that first summer day. There was something else linked to that time and place, something that she must not forget. But at the

Melyukovs', a circle game was starting now, a rollicking game that used a ring, a string, and a silver coin. Whatever it was that she had to remember could surely wait until later . . .

A fierce whisper from a small Turk brought her back to earth.

"Anne! Where is the guy you were chasing? Where's the book?" One hand was on his scimitar, and his blond hair stuck out from under his tea-towel turban.

It was Will. Hovering just behind him was a short Tartar who turned out to be Emily.

Everything came back to Anne then—the garden party, the interloper, the book opening to a blank page as she called desperately for help—yes, she remembered it all now, but with a kind of detachment, as though it had happened to someone else.

"We only just made it," Emily was saying breathlessly, hoisting up the baggy trousers under her caftan. "Oh, Anne, we almost lost you."

They had dashed into the library just in time to be sucked into the whirlwind. They had seen the interloper's dark coattails flying, and Anne holding on for dear life. Will had managed to grab her green skirt as she whipped by, and Emily had caught his other hand when he was pulled after Anne. The next thing they knew they were tumbling through snow, on and on for ages until they landed here.

"It's doing opposites now, isn't it?" Emily remarked brightly, taking in the fireplace, the snow that gleamed through the ballroom's dark windows, and the enchanting Christmas tree straight out of *Nutcracker*. "You know, from an August garden party in America to a Christmas costume party in Russia."

"Actually, it's New Year's Eve," Anne said, a little cross that they had interrupted her, and a little sorry that she felt that way. "See that box of snow? Before the mummers arrived—that's us, and all these other people wearing costumes—well, the Melyukovs were pouring melted wax into the snow to see what shadows the shapes would cast on the wall. It's one way of foretelling the future on the last night of the year."

How did I know that? she wondered. *It must be in the book.*

"The book!" Will said again, too stubborn to be distracted by all this chatter. "Where's the book? And where's the bad guy with the beard? He must be around here somewhere, too."

With a shiver like the crack in a mirror, Anne reluctantly pulled herself away from Natasha's story in *War and Peace* and back to her own.

Now she recalled what the interloper had said about the book's power. What had he called it? Something *Hermetica*. Perhaps it was true that the book did not belong in their world. Perhaps it should never have been on a shelf in the Queens Public Library, or in the hands of three children quarreling their way through a summer vacation. But it certainly did not belong to a grasping, wolfish man who talked about dominion over the earth. And if they did not take it back from him, who would?

There were many beards in the crowd, some real and some false. There were tall, hooded figures and large furry ones. So Anne, Will, and Emily scanned the masqueraders for yellow eyes, and tried to puzzle out the magic logic that had brought such a creature into their garden in the first place, sniffing the air for the book's scent.

It was easier to guess why the book had brought them here. It seemed that their combined thoughts of winter and Russians and cold war had been strong enough to draw Tolstoy's world into the blank endleaf that the interloper had used to unleash his whirlwind. But unless they could find him soon, he would surely find a way to move on alone, taking the book with him.

"*And who is this?*" stout Mrs. Melyukov asked, peering at Emily and laughing into her handkerchief. "*I suppose it is one of the Rostovs. Well, Mr. Hussar, and what regiment do you serve in?"* she asked Anne. *"Here, hand some fruit jelly to the Turk!"* she ordered the butler, *who was passing round refreshments. "That's not forbidden by his law."*

The fruit jelly was delicious, Will found, with a cool, curranty taste that made him hungry for the supper being laid out in the next room. Might as well look for the wolf guy in there, he told the others. Might as well get a bite to eat while they could.

The musicians changed from a waltz to a carol, not a familiar one, like "I Saw Three Ships" or "The Holly and the Ivy," but a riddle song. The words made Will think of one of the ballads his mother loved to sing. This one was different, he thought, yet the same.

A man stops at a garden and sees a young girl. *Shall I ask thee riddles, beauteous maiden? / Six wise riddles shall I ask thee?* Yes, she replies. *Well then, maiden, what is higher than the forest? / Also, what is brighter than the light? / Also, maiden, what is thicker than the forest?*

There were so many ballads and so many different versions of each one, you could never be sure when a stranger in a garden was going to turn out to be somebody's true love, or a demon lover who had to be outwitted, or even the ghost of a long-lost brother, Will thought. But he had a special affection for riddles now, and he tried to catch some of the answers in this version amid the clatter of the supper table.

Higher than the forest is the moon . . . Thicker than the forest are the stars . . . Never silent, stranger, is the sea . . .

Over supper the Melyukovs talked about fortune-telling and divination. The end of the year was a special time for it, it seemed, almost a point outside of time, when uncanny beings could be summoned and hidden treasures revealed. A mirror in moonlight, a table set for two in a bathhouse, even the silence of an empty barn could conjure up the image of one's future bridegroom—or summon up a demonic spirit disguised in his shape. But woe to the young girl who looked behind her, or covered her eyes in fright. She had to keep the creature talking until the cock crowed, when all spells would be broken, or she would be dragged to the underworld herself.

Did none of the girls want to try their fate with a solitary visit to the barn? someone asked. And amid the squeals of horrified delight, Anne suddenly knew what she must do.

"I'll go," she declared, to Emily and Will's consternation.

There was a hubbub of reaction.

"Oh, it's a terrifying thing, trying one's fate in a barn," warned an elderly maiden aunt who lived with the Melyukovs.

"Tell her what happened to that young lady," put in one of the Melyukov daughters.

"Well, it was like this," the elderly woman began as a hush fell over the company. "The young lady took a mirror to the empty barn. After sitting alone a little while, she heard a sleigh with bells driving up. Then she heard a sound at the door. And all of a sudden, there he is, in the shape of a man. And he sits right down beside her."

Gasps and stifled screams ran round the table. "But what did he do?" asked another guest. "Did he talk like a man?"

"Yes, exactly like a man, and tried to win her over," the old aunt went on. "She should have kept him talking till the cock crowed. She should have watched him only in her mirror, and never turned to see him at all. But she got frightened—simply took fright, and hid her face in her hands. Then he had his chance, and grabbed her. Luckily, the maids ran in . . ."

"Come, why are you scaring them?" Mrs. Melyukov protested. "Now none of them will go."

"I'll go," Anne said again, getting up. "I'm not afraid. I'll go right now."

Before Will or Emily could intervene, the old aunt and several maidservants had clustered around Anne, all offering warnings and advice. They gave her directions to the empty barn, and told her to stand quite silent and listen when she got there. Someone fetched a fur cloak, and helped her muffle up against the cold. Then the old aunt herself brought Anne a small mirror from the next room, and carefully wrapped it up in a white napkin together with a candlestick and a few matches. On no condition was Anne to look away from the mirror, the old lady kept repeating, no matter what the reflection revealed, and no matter how frightening the apparition.

As soon as Anne stepped out into the corridor, Emily and Will ran after her.

"What are you doing?" Emily demanded. "We were supposed to stay together!"

"Don't worry, I have a plan," Anne told them. "I'm sure this is what the magic intended. Don't you see? It's a chance to draw the bad guy out, to trap him and take back the book."

They stood whispering together in a hurried council of war. Emily proposed a backup rescue strategy, Will, a quick-getaway scheme. The scenario still felt very risky, but it might work, they agreed.

Then Anne made her way out of the house alone.

"Straight, straight, along the path, miss," the oldest maidservant called out after her. *"Only, don't look back."*

＊

On the snow outside, the full moon shone so bright that the bare lime trees cast tangled shadows at Anne's feet. Once, she heard a branch snap with frost in the cold stillness; then all was silent again. The dark sky was sprinkled with stars. They seemed faint and far away beside the sparkling diamonds of moonlight in the snow. In the distance, beyond the log barn, she could see the snow-covered mass of the forest. There in the darkness, not in the bright house or moonlit garden, the interloper must be lurking.

"The moon on the breast of the new-fallen snow / Gave the lustre of mid-day to objects below," she whispered to herself for comfort, as though she were still little enough to be looking for Santa Claus, instead of luring a stranger who looked like a wolf.

This time and place were not of his choosing, Anne was sure. This was a detour, imposed on him not only by the magic and their own longings but by the power of the words a great writer had placed on a blank page a century ago. Now the interloper, impatient to get away, would be tempted to try to bend the same power to his ends. It was up to them to beat him at his own game.

WOLVES IN THE SNOW

𝒯he empty barn smelled of damp wood and hay dust.
Anne closed the creaking door, but left it unlatched. She
held her breath for a moment. It was not really dark inside
once her eyes got used to the gloom. Moonlight seeped
through the cracks between the logs, and spilled through
a small, high opening cut under the roof. She soon found
a knothole that let her look out toward the forest.

Yes, there it was already, a dark shape detaching itself from the mass of trees. It was loping, almost running, toward the barn. Quick, quick, she told herself, trying to unwrap the mirror and the candlestick and not to drop them in her haste. She fumbled with the matches, breaking the first one and seeing the second sputter out. Finally the last match flared and caught.

Anne set the flickering candle at the center of the bare floorboards, as the old aunt had instructed. She stood beside it, listening, and gazed past her own pale face into the depths of the looking glass. Her back was turned to the door. She watched the door's reflection, waiting for the moment when it would creak open.

First came a footfall outside, and a cracking sound, and then, for an instant, the moonlight from the opening doorway dazzled her. It took all her concentration not to turn around. Tilting the mirror, she saw the silhouette of a man step over the threshold.

But he was not what she had expected. This man was young and handsome, she saw with surprise. His face was shaven smooth except for a becoming hint of stubble above lips that curled into a winning smile. When he threw back his fur-lined cloak with one hand, she glimpsed a fine white shirt and the gleam of a silver belt buckle. Even in the gloom, in the mirror, she could tell that his eyes were the color of a summer twilight.

"Shall I ask thee riddles, beauteous maiden?" He was half singing, half whispering the question from the Russian song. And Anne, confused now as she stared at his reflection, answered with more confidence than she felt: "Yes, please."

※

On the other side of the vast house, beside the lantern-lit stables where a lone horse boy slumbered, Emily and Will were trying to pick out a suitable getaway sleigh from those left tied outside. Emily liked the first one in the row, a red-trimmed sledge pulled by big black stallions. Will leaned to the second, a blue sledge drawn by dappled bays. Then they saw the third, and knew it for their own. The silvery sleigh bed was harnessed to a black, a chestnut, and a bay, and the mismatched trio were tossing their proud heads as though in assent. Will and Emily both reached for the reins.

"It's still too soon, Emily," Will hissed.

"No, it isn't," Emily argued. "Let's ride to the barn now."

Luckily, the horses were untroubled by the brief tug of war. But the tinkling of harness bells reminded the children that any real movement would be heard for miles. Working together, they began feverishly unbuckling the leather straps that held the rows of bells in place.

"I'll never feel the same about 'Jingle Bells,' " Emily said crossly, her fingers stiff from the cold.

"Say, that reminds me," Will whispered. "You know that song they were singing inside? That riddle song? Don't you think it was kind of like that song Mom sings about the stranger and the three children, the one about Old Nick?"

"Mmm-hmm," Emily said absently, her mind on the last and tightest buckle, and on sorting out the mix of resentment and relief she felt that it was Anne in the barn instead of her. Then, as often happened to Emily, the echo of the last words to be spoken seemed to catch up with her brain. A worried look crossed her face.

"Wait a minute, Will. Say that again."

She, too, suddenly remembered the raw, rainy Saturday afternoon when their mother first sang them a riddle ballad. Anne wasn't there. She was in the city with Grandmother Thornton, having a lunch at Schrafts and a visit to the Frick Museum, where children under ten were not admitted. Emily had been miserable—"green with envy," her mother called it. Grandmother, who believed in giving a special treat to one grandchild at a time, described the Frick as a storybook mansion with a fountain inside and some of the world's loveliest paintings. Just the fact that it was closed to Emily because of her age made it unbearably enticing. For Will the matter was simpler, but no less infuriating: he wanted one of the ice cream sundaes that were a Schrafts specialty.

To comfort them as the gray afternoon wore on, their mother made cocoa and toasted English muffins. She sang the scary riddle song while the milk was warming, before heading back to the typewriter to revise her column about medieval herbs for modern times.

There was a lady in the West,
Lay the bank with the bonny broom
She had three children of the best.
Down the dale, dilly down doom

There came a stranger to the gate,
(Lay the bank with the bonny broom)
And he three days and nights did wait.
(Down the dale, dilly down doom)

The eldest child did ope' the door,
The second set him on the floor.
The third child brought the stranger a chair,
And placed it that he might sit there.

"Now answer me these questions three,
Or you shall surely go with me.

"Now answer me these questions six,
Or you shall surely be Old Nick's.

"Now answer me these questions nine,
Or you shall surely all be mine.

"What is greener than the grass?
What is smoother than crystal glass?

"What is louder than a horn?
What is sharper than a thorn?

"What is brighter than the light?
What is darker than the night?

"What is keener than an axe?
What is softer than melting wax?

"What is rounder than a ring?"
"To you we thus our answers bring."

Now, standing in the cold, Emily and Will remembered the smell of hot chocolate and the cozy sound of their mother's voice in the kitchen. Just then the moon went behind a cloud, and a gust of wind skittered across the snow crust. They both shivered.

"I bet the song's not just an accident," Will said, peering behind the house toward the barn and, beyond it, at the icy path polished by sleigh runners that led into the forest. "I bet that wolf guy is coming to ask Anne riddles. You know, sort of like a contest for the book?"

"But she doesn't know the answers!" Emily moaned. "C'mon!"

And jumping into the silenced sleigh, they set off for the barn as fast as the horses would go.

The sleigh path veered away from the house in a great semicircle before it forked, one branch looping back to the far side of the log barn, the other branch arcing toward the forest. Wind whistled past their ears, and snow spray stung their faces. Just as they were reaching the fork, more clouds scudded across the sky and blotted out half the stars.

It began to snow. Blinking the thick flakes from her eyelashes, Emily thought she saw a light glitter inside the barn. Together she and Will pulled the horses to a stop at the side of the building, and Emily leaped out. While Will held the reins, she groped along the snow-covered log wall with bare fingers until she found a chink big enough to look through.

"I can see him," Emily called softly. "I think he's holding the book behind his back. But I can't see Anne."

"Let me look," Will demanded.

"No!" she said. "You've got to stay with the sleigh and be ready to drive us away as soon as Anne runs out."

"But where is she?" he asked. "I think we should jump him now and grab the book while we have the chance."

"Shh, I'm going to try to listen." Emily crept around to the door in her fur-lined boots, holding the hood of her cloak nearly closed against the snow. It was falling faster now, blowing in great gusts against the barn.

Anne's voice came through the crack in the door in a thin, dreamy singsong, hardly sounding like Anne at all.

"Envy is greener than the grass,
Flattery smoother than crystal glass.

"Rumour is louder than a horn,
Hunger is sharper than a thorn.

"Truth is brighter than the light,
Falsehood is darker than the night . . ."

But at the word *night* her voice faltered and trailed off.

What was keener than an axe? What was softer than melting wax? What was rounder than a ring?

In the darkening barn, Anne's mind had gone as blank of answers as an empty page. And in the shadows of the mirror that she held, she could see the stranger's charming smile spread into a smirk.

"A little knowledge," he whispered, "is a dangerous thing."

Anne felt her hands begin to tremble. As the mirror quivered, the stranger's face seemed to shift and slide in the reflection. The shadow of a stubble was spreading from his upper lip to his whole jaw, to his neck, even over his ears. And those eyes! Not dusky blue, after all, but the glowing yellow gaze of a wolf waiting for her in the dark.

Anne screamed and turned to confront him. At the same moment, Emily wrenched open the door. She threw herself against the stranger's back, and knocked the book from his grasp. There was a frantic scrabbling for it on the barn floor, a growling, yelping, shrieking tangle of arms and legs and fur.

Outside, hearing Anne's scream above the rising wind, Will dropped the reins and tore around the corner. He skidded into the barn on his icy boots, just in time to kick the book from the clawing reach of a hand in a fingerless glove. The book spun on the worn wooden floorboards, skipped on a loose nail, and slid to a stop beside Anne. She seized it with both hands.

Instantly, she remembered. The words almost chanted themselves, as quickly as her tongue could say them. On the last lines, Emily and Will joined in.

"Revenge is keener than an axe,
Love is softer than melting wax.

"The world is rounder than a ring,
To you we thus our answers bring.

"Thus you have our answers nine,
And we NEVER shall be thine."

A howl of rage filled the barn. The children did not wait to savor their triumph. Dodging out the door, they ran together through the falling snow. They skittered around the corner of the building, half afraid that the sleigh would be gone. But no, there it was, with the horses stamping and snorting clouds of steam—the black, the chestnut, and the dappled bay, all raring to go. They took off at a trot the moment the children threw themselves into the sleigh bed, without waiting for anyone to take the reins. Soon they were galloping through the woods, with Anne, Emily, and Will tumbled together in the fur blankets.

"We did it!" Emily exulted. "Is the book okay? I hope it wasn't hurt by that kick Will gave it." She leaned closer, putting a hand on the small volume in Anne's lap. But Anne quickly thrust the book inside her cloak.

"I don't think we should start gloating yet," she said. "We'd better get as far away as we can before we turn to the book. I have a feeling it's not going to be that simple."

For reasons she could not begin to explain to Emily, or even to herself, she also wanted a moment to hold the book close and think over what had happened in the barn.

That young man with eyes like twilight—was he nothing but a phantom, conjured up by the interloper out of the romantic bits from her favorite books to trap her? Or was he a real person, a guest from her future, borrowed as a disguise?

Even now, she liked to remember the bow he had made when she had said yes to the riddle game. Even now, she wanted to replay the way he had straightened up and met her eyes in the mirror, and then laughed—not a sinister laugh, surely, but a laugh of recognition.

"Anne," he had said. "Why, it's you!"

But when she asked his name, he only put one finger to his lips and shook his head. And then, instead of the six riddles from the Russian carol, he had asked her the nine questions from the English ballad that her mother used to sing right after Will was born, when Anne was the only one of the three children old enough to begin to understand it.

The smell of old wood in the barn, the soft fur of her own cloak against her cheek, the gentle singsong of words she knew but had forgotten—oh, if she could only capture and keep that one moment, she would surely understand everything! But it was already slipping away in the rushing shadows of the trees and the white billows of the driving snow.

"Is this the way home?" Will asked. His voice had a little quaver in it now.

"The horses seem to know where they're going," Emily said. But at that very moment she noticed that the two side horses were sinking into the deep drifts, leaning against the shafts of the middle horse, barely able to stay on the path.

"It's like the song," Emily added hopefully, singing it into the wind. *"Over the river and through the woods, / To Grandmother's house we go. / The horse knows the way to carry the sleigh / O'er the deep and drifting sno-ow!"*

"But *our* grandmother doesn't live here," Will said. He was thinking of Grandmother Thornton's apartment building in Manhattan, of the shiny brass buttons in the elevator, and the faint smell of furniture polish and mothballs when she opened the door. He was remembering framed pictures of his father as a little boy, and the sizzling sound of roasting chicken, and how later, when they drove back over the bridge, he would fall asleep in the car and wake to feel his father carrying him up to bed.

"I want to go home," Will said.

Anne and Emily glanced at each other. They recognized the ominous note in Will's voice. It was a tone that, if ignored, was often followed by tears or a tantrum. He was a brave and resourceful little kid, but he was still a little kid, and it was very late now and very cold.

"If this is *War and Peace*," Emily asked Anne, trying to sound casual, "where are we going?"

Anne could only shake her head. She had started the novel one rainy day in early August. But the Russian names kept changing from one paragraph to the next, and she had soon lost her way. She remembered the relief she had felt at her father's words—*Don't rush it, kiddo. Like most of life's good things, it's worth waiting for.* Fleetingly, Anne realized that those words applied to her mysterious stranger, too. Perhaps, when she was older . . . Meanwhile, she had no idea where the horses were heading. The snow was falling too fast and thick now even to see where they'd been.

Looking back, Anne saw a blur of white against darkness, and a ghostly path through the trees. The wind rattled snow from the highest branches, then died down again like the ebb between waves in the sea. And just before the next gust, she caught a new sound in the distance behind them: the crack of a whip, and a cry of pursuit.

"He's coming after us," she said.

Fear seized hold of them then.

The wolf guy, Will had called him. They had all avoided dwelling on the implications. But when Will was younger, he had been so afraid of wolves, or rather of The Wolf, that Emily, especially, could not resist tormenting him with scary stories. There was the wolf who ate Little Red Riding Hood, of course, and the one who ate the duck in *Peter and the Wolf*. There was the wolf who ate the seven kids while their mother was away, after disguising his voice with chalk and persuading them to open the door. But worst of all was the werewolf Emily had made up herself once, when they were on a walk with their mother on a dead-end street.

"You know why they call it dead end?" Emily had whispered malevolently to then-four-year-old Will, just as a thunderstorm began to rumble. "This is where dead people are buried. And one of them is turning into a werewolf right NOW."

Will shrieked and ran—and later forgot all about it. Emily, on the other hand, still thought of werewolves every time she heard distant thunder or saw a sign that read DEAD END. Sometimes, just before falling asleep, she would jerk awake again with the conviction that the werewolf she had made up to frighten Will had come to life and was clawing at her door.

Now there was a clutching of hands in the sleigh as the three children peered back through the snow into the deeper woods. What were those shadows passing between the tree trunks? Was it just the speed of the sleigh that gave them an illusion of motion? Or were those really dark, beastlike shapes streaking against the white ground?

"Wolves," Will said in a husky voice, naming what Emily and Anne were still hoping was their imagination. "The wolves are after us, too."

That explained why the horses were running faster than ever without a driver or a whip to spur them on. Nostrils flaring, eyes wide with fear, they put on another burst of speed as the loping shapes drew closer.

"The book, oh, quick, Anne, the book," Emily cried. But Anne, who had been fumbling with it under her cloak for some time, already knew that her hunch was right. The book had been wrenched to the interloper's purpose, then stalled and battered between opposing forces. It would no longer work as an easy door back to the August night of their parents' garden party. It would not open in her hands at all.

"Here, you try," she said in despair, pulling the book

from her cloak and handing it to Emily. Neither she nor Will could pry it open, try as they might, turning the book this way and that way as the sleigh rocked and shook.

And then the howling began. First a single, wild note rising above the rattle of the speeding sleigh, and then the answering howls, some so far away they were almost lost in the whistle of the wind, some so close the children instinctively shrank back and clung to one another.

"Gee up, my lovelies!" came another cry, not far behind them. The words were those a man might use to encourage his team through a snowstorm. But the deep, rasping voice was the interloper's, and all three children realized at the same moment that he was not calling to his horses. He was calling to the wolves.

The horses began to flag. They could smell the pack behind them, but even terror could no longer give them the strength for more speed. The snowstorm was dying down, and the loping shapes now stood out more starkly. Their eyes gleamed in the dark as they converged from both sides of the path, less than a hundred yards behind the sleigh, and gaining.

Just when all seemed lost, the road ahead straightened out and broke clear of the trees. The horses hurtled from the woods into an open landscape. A last, fierce gust of wind swept the clouds from the moon. Suddenly, silvery light bathed a vast expanse of new-fallen snow, flat and white and empty as far as the eye could see.

There was no road to follow now, not even a footpath. But it didn't seem to matter. The sleigh runners sliced through the powdery snow as though it were sugar, sliding so fast that the sleigh seemed to fly. There was ice under the snow, Anne thought, smoother by far than the rutted road through the woods. No bumps now, no shaking, just the muffled rhythm of the horses' hooves flying on and on, leaving the howling behind.

And then, quite abruptly, the horses slowed and came to a stop. Only breathing broke the stillness now. Scanning ahead for landmarks, the children saw nothing—not a hillock, not a tree, just the flat, glittering field of white stretching to the horizon. Looking back, they saw the marks of the horses' hooves and the grooves left by the sleigh runners, but only for a moment. Even as they watched, a small sigh of wind over snowdrifts erased their tracks.

I've been here before, Anne thought.

She remembered her father's voice in the car at night, and the mesmerizing beams of the highway lights passing to and fro like the hands of a metronome. A long winter trip in a foreign country years ago, with the others fast asleep in the back, even her mother, who had dozed off af-

ter nursing baby Will. "Is that a field or a lake?" her father
had muttered to himself. And as though he had asked her
a riddle, she piped up, "Tell me, Daddy."

"Have I ever told you the story of the Writer across
Lake Constance?" he asked. Or at least that was what she
heard. She was just mastering the written alphabet then,
so when he spoke of a messenger with an important message to deliver, she imagined writing the letters herself in
very black ink on a white page.

The Writer turned into a Rider, a messenger who
mounted his horse and rode as fast as he could through a
bitter cold night. He rode and he rode, watching for the
shore of the lake where a ferryman's boat would carry him
and his horse to the other side. Instead, he kept riding
over snow-covered fields in the dark, never meeting a
soul, hearing only the cracking of icy ground and his
horse's pounding hooves. Finally, near daybreak, he came
to a village. How much farther to Lake Constance?
he asked. "Why, it's behind you," the startled villagers
replied. And looking back in the first light of day, he saw
that the snowy field he had crossed was really an immense
frozen lake. The cracking under his horse's hooves had
been thin ice. At every step he had been in mortal danger
of sinking into the dark waters below. And the thought so
frightened him that he fell down dead.

"But what about the message?" Anne had asked her father.

He laughed, and her mother shushed them, so Anne never did get an answer. Instead she fell asleep, and dreamed of big black, watery letters spreading across a field of snow just like this one.

Thinking hard now, Anne glanced up at the sky. It was paler, and the moon was fading. Nearly daybreak, the time when all spells would be broken, according to the Russian fortune-telling tales. Was the ice under the snow one more spell, perhaps the last twist in the interloper's sorcery? He had driven them far out on a frozen lake, knowing that the ice would crack open and dissolve beneath them with the first rays of the sun.

Anne jumped from the sleigh. All around her she saw the snow waiting, like the empty page of the book that had swept them here. She leaned over. In one hand she clutched the closed book. With the other, she swept through the snow to the darker ice below—up and down and around, awkwardly at first and then more smoothly as her arm found the rhythm of the words in her head.

Emily and Will, looking down from the sleigh, saw the letters take shape just as dawn gleamed on the horizon: *And then Anne, Emily, and Will were back home safe and sound again.*

*

The children sprawled onto the rug in the library. August heat washed over them, more welcome to their cold limbs than a fur blanket in a snowstorm. The house was still overflowing with music and chatter.

"What are you three doing here on the floor?" their father asked. "Run along now. Mingle a little. I have to make a long-distance phone call."

Anne felt around on the floor. "Here it is," she said triumphantly. "Look."

The book lay open. She pointed to the last line at the bottom of the page. "And then Anne, Emily, and Will were back home safe and sound again."

"But how—" began Emily.

"But what about—" broke in Will.

"Go on, scram," their father said. And this time, they took the hint.

DATE DUE: TODAY

𝕿he next morning, the heat had broken. A west wind brought a high blue sky and a crisp rustling in the trees, almost like fall. It reminded Anne of the smell of new school shoes wrapped in rustling tissue paper, and the crisp feel of a new notebook when you turn the pages for the first time. She stretched, and felt a surge of energy.

"I wonder if he watched us disappear," Emily said from

her side of the room. "You know, gnashing his teeth and twisting his mustache, and saying, 'Foiled again,' like in the silent movies."

"That's not the way I see it," Anne began. But before she could say how she *did* see it, her father's voice bellowed from below: "Anne! Get down here. This is unforgivable!"

While chasing spilled olive pits and bits of a broken wineglass, he had found the library copy of *War and Peace* lying open under the couch, facedown. "That is no way to treat a book," he told her, turning it over and cradling the spine. Then he glanced down at the open pages, and his face softened in recognition. He had not read the passage for years, but it was one of his favorites—when Natasha, Sonya, and Nikolai arrive by sleigh at the Melyukovs' party, in disguise.

"Who is it?" asked someone from the porch.

"The mummers from the count's. I know by the horses," *other voices replied.*

Catching himself, he frowned again and turned to the inside front cover. "And it was due yesterday," he scolded.

"Honest, I don't know how it got there," Anne told him. "I'll take it back today."

"Take them all back after breakfast," their mother put in. "Didn't you kids check out a basketful of books at the start of the summer? Time to clear the decks. Just one more week to go before school starts."

As they left to collect the other books, their father was still holding the copy of *War and Peace*, weighing it thoughtfully in his hands.

"Elizabeth, what do you know about werewolves?" he asked. "I didn't have a chance to tell you last night, but when I reached Gordon again, he told me the damnedest story."

After that, you could hardly blame the children for lingering outside the door to listen. They caught only a few phrases at first: "Found Donderberg delirious . . . maybe a concussion . . . kept talking about . . ."

Then their mother's voice, incredulous, rose to a shriek. "A werewolf sorcerer?" she cried. "John, are we talking about your veteran correspondent, Daniel David tough-as-nails Donderberg?"

Their father shushed her. "Not so loud," he said. "Shows what stress can do to the best of us. Of course Gordon has always been excitable, but he says old Donder's really unhinged. Keeps raving about war and peace and keeping children safe. I ordered them both home for some rest."

Anne slipped back into the room and hovered discreetly behind a wing chair.

"The weirdest part," she heard her father add, "is that Donderberg is convinced he sent this werewolf to our garden party by mistake. I mean, can you believe it? I told Gordon the only party animal who showed up here last night was an *artiste* who decided to swim with the goldfish."

Their mother giggled. "Well, it *was* hot," she said. "And Zenia believes that indulging impulses is good for artistic vision. But where on earth did Donderberg pick up this werewolf notion?"

"I guess it all started when he missed his train connection in Transylvania, and tried to hike through the woods to the next station. He stumbled on some bearded local who took him home for the night. Mr. Werewolf, I presume."

"Oh, John," Anne's mother said, dissolving into helpless laughter. "I just hope the paper can keep it quiet. Poor Donder! He'll be so embarrassed when he snaps out of it."

✳

The children talked it over later in hushed voices as they packed up the library basket.

"I feel like I'm missing half the story," Emily complained, stacking *War and Peace* at the bottom with the biggest books.

"Maybe magic works something like an electric current," Anne said slowly. "Or like sound waves. Remember how Dad and I both picked up the telephone when that missing reporter called from Transylvania? I think the interloper was on the line, too. I bet he got the current or the echo of the book, somehow, and then wormed useful bits of information about us from Donderberg. I bet his sorcery relied on the book's own power—like judo, sort of, only different."

Will wedged a large, slim book at the side of the basket. "Do you think the wolf guy will try again?" he asked.

"No," Anne said firmly. "He won't. Or at least not with us."

She put the small, faded volume on top of the pile in the basket. It looked a little the worse for wear. There was a tiny blot on the cover, maybe from melted snowflakes, Anne thought. Emily, touching the same spot, thought it was a smudge of leaf mold from Sherwood Forest. Will figured it was just a little garden grass stain, albeit from a blade as big as a small tree. They all sighed.

Will opened the cover to check the library stamp one more time. "Date Due: Today," it said. Just to be sure, he tried to turn the pages. Just to be sure, Anne and Emily each tried, too. Not a single flutter. And still the purple stamp silently called for the book's return.

"It isn't fair," Emily protested halfheartedly. "What if

it falls into the wrong hands? I mean, all those extra powers that we haven't even had a chance to try, like, what did the wolfman call it, dominion over time and earth . . ."

"Emily," her sister said severely. "Don't be greedy."

A few heated words were exchanged then, but by the time they set out for the library, peace prevailed.

They didn't talk much. The new school year was looming in their thoughts when they reached the library. Will was imagining the surprised faces of the other kids after his second-grade teacher called on him to read aloud. Emily was wondering whether Belinda Popper had cut off her braids at summer camp and curled her bangs, and if she would be too unbearably stuck up to sit next to at lunch if she had. Anne was remembering an unused school notebook stashed at the bottom of her sweater drawer.

They were already standing on the library steps, ready to tug at the front door, when they realized it was locked.

"Rats! The library's closed," Emily said. "And I really wanted to check out *The Midnight Folk*. Belinda Popper had the nerve to write me from camp that it's too scary for me. Ha! If she only knew."

Slowly, they fed the books through the return slot, one at a time, listening for the inevitable thud at the other end of the chute. Finally only one book was left to go.

"I can't bear to do it," Emily said. "Can you?"

"I think it should be Will," Anne said. She held open the slot. Standing on his toes, Will took the small, nondescript volume in both hands and tipped it in.

They all waited for the thud. But there was only silence.

On the way home, Anne considered that silence. Of course, it wasn't really silence at all, she thought. There was the rustle of leaves in the big old library maple. The squeak of Will's sneakers when he fell back on his heels. Their own quiet breathing. And yes, a kind of expectant echo from inside the library, as if the books, row upon row of them on the dusky shelves, were still waiting.

Lying in the green hammock later, she could almost hear them. And opening her notebook in the dusk, she began to write.

ACKNOWLEDGMENTS

Happily, most of the books that filled the children's library basket can still be found in print, including, of course, Leo Tolstoy's *War and Peace*. But the "immense, illustrated edition" of Tolstoy's masterpiece that Anne brought home from the library is my own invention. The lines I put in italics on pages 187, 191–92 (top), and 195 are passages taken directly from Tolstoy's chapters 142 and 143, but they draw on three different English translations of the Russian text, and so differ slightly from all published versions. In weaving together Anne's story with Natasha's and then Sonya's, I made liberal use of Tolstoy's description of the Melyukov party, its dinner table discussion about fortune-telling, and the girls' efforts at divination. But I freely changed phrases and details to suit my story, while trying to be faithful to nineteenth-century accounts of Russian folk beliefs.

Except for the Gnomblins' rune, which is original, the ballads the children heard and recited are real ballads, ones that were passed on orally for centuries before anyone wrote them down. Singers through the ages have changed lines to suit themselves and their audiences; I did, too, so my versions will not exactly match those published previously. I mainly drew on variants of "Willie and Earl Richard's Daughter," about Robin Hood's birth; "Thomas Rhymer" (which others call Thomas the Rhymer or True Thomas); and "Riddles Wisely Expounded." All were collected in the late nineteenth century by Francis J. Child, published in five volumes titled *The English and Scottish Popular Ballads*, and now are known simply as Child Ballads. On my pages 192 (bottom) and 193 I also quote (with small changes) a Russian riddle song that Child cites in translation from W. R. Ralston's 1872 book, *Songs of the Russian People*. On page 177 I quote Irving Berlin's song "I've Got My Love to Keep Me Warm."

Will's favorite insect book is partly modeled on *Familiar Insects and Spiders* (The Audubon Society Pocket Guides; 1988), which was a great help in describing the ten-times-too-big creatures of Jardinia. Lines from Will's favorite story, "Jack and the Beanstalk," are from Joseph Jacobs's version in *English Fairy Tales* (1890).

The words that whispered through the glen when Anne realized she was in Sherwood Forest are from the 1902 poem "Sherwood," by Alfred Noyes. Like me, Anne had first read them in *The Adventures of Robin Hood*, collected and retold by Roger Lancelyn Green in a paperback published by Penguin in 1956.

A different kind of acknowledgment is due to the children my sons used to be: Daniel, with his boundless zest for outdoor adventures of his own invention, and David, who declared himself my editor the summer he was nine, and listened, with encouraging enthusiasm, to day-by-day installments of the Thornton children's story. My special thanks also go to my sister, Lynn, who provided a more critical reading, with suggestions that were still valuable when finally—with fresh encouragement from a grown-up David—I finished the manuscript.

Throughout, I was inspired by the works of Edward Eager and his inimitable way with bookish children, mystifying magic, even an enchanted library book due back in seven days. In the end, many books influenced the way I told the story of Anne, Emily, and Will Thornton, but none more than the plots that Lynn and I concocted and played with our brothers, Paul and Danny, in another garden many years ago. In memory of those games, and those children, this book is dedicated to the magic we found at the library.